"And now I'm the one coming to the rescue."

He quirked a grin at her.

She kept her facial expression controlled and didn't smile back. "I won't deny I hope that's the case. It would help him a tremendous amount knowing he's no longer responsible for it, even though most of the day-to-day operations fall on me, and to an extent, Aunt Anna."

"Well, I like what I've seen so far. The store has a tremendous amount of potential, and it's better organized than either of the other two stores I own."

"Tomorrow you can spend the day looking over the books and inventory lists and anything else you need. I'll help however I can." She smoothed down her apron, then looked him full in the face. "My goal, Joseph, is to convince you this store is worth purchasing."

"Then we see eye to eye." He couldn't help himself. "All forgiven?"

She startled, and a hard expression came into her eyes. It was clear she knew exactly what he meant.

"No," she said low. "It's not."

Living on a remote self-sufficient homestead in North Idaho, **Patrice Lewis** is a Christian wife, mother, author, blogger, columnist and speaker. She has practiced and written about rural subjects for almost thirty years. When she isn't writing, Patrice enjoys self-sufficiency projects, such as animal husbandry, small-scale dairy production, gardening, food preservation and canning, and homeschooling. She and her husband have been married since 1990 and have two daughters.

Books by Patrice Lewis

Love Inspired

Visit the Author Profile page at LoveInspired.com.

The Quilter's Scandalous Past

Patrice Lewis

LOVE INSPIRED

INSPIRATIONAL ROMANCE

LOVE INSPIRED®

INSPIRATIONAL ROMANCE

Recycling programs
for this product may
not exist in your area.

ISBN-13: 978-1-335-58567-7

The Quilter's Scandalous Past

Copyright © 2023 by Patrice Lewis

For questions and comments about the quality of this book, please contact us at CustomerService@Harlequin.com.

Love Inspired
22 Adelaide St. West, 41st Floor
Toronto, Ontario M5H 4E3, Canada
www.LoveInspired.com

Printed in U.S.A.

And forgive us our debts, as we forgive our debtors.
—*Matthew* 6:12

To God, for blessing me with my husband and daughters, the best family anyone could hope for.

Chapter One

The June afternoon in Chaffinch, Indiana, was warm and lovely. Esther Yoder paused as a meadowlark perched on a fence post right outside her office window. The bird warbled its beautiful song, then departed with a flutter.

She smiled, regretting she couldn't be outside on such a pretty day. But she had work to do and a store to manage. Ledger books full of numbers were spread out on the wooden desk before her.

At least the town was quiet enough that meadowlarks could serenade through an open window. The last of the tour buses had departed for the day, taking with them the *Englisch* visitors who came from far and near to experience an Amish town.

And as always, Esther was right there to greet them as they came into her aunt and uncle's huge emporium. The business had begun as a supplier of dry goods for Amish and other Plain People, but over the years, it had morphed into a large mercantile, educational venue and tourist destination in the heart of Indiana's Amish country.

But for now, the town center was quiet. Esther bent her head once more over the figures in front of her.

Aunt Anna entered the small office. "I've got good news, Esther."

"What is it, *aenti*?" Esther laid down her pencil, pleased at an excuse to stop crunching numbers. She smiled at the older woman, whose gray hair was tucked neatly under her *kapp*.

"It looks like we may have a buyer for the store." Anna grinned.

"Really!" Esther jumped to her feet, toppling her ledger book onto the floor as she embraced her aunt. "That's wonderful news! Praise *Gott*! Does Uncle Paul know?"

"Yes, he spoke to the man earlier. Paul is so happy. It will be a chance for him to rest and get his health back."

"When? How long before he takes it over? How early can he be here? How did you find a buyer?" Esther nearly babbled in her excitement.

Anna laughed, a sound of pure relief. "He knows your parents, and they mentioned we wanted to sell the store because of your uncle's health. Apparently, the man owns two other Amish stores in different parts of Indiana, so he's experienced at running them."

"Is he *Englisch*?"

"No, Amish. But he's quite a businessman, apparently. He chooses his investments carefully, and he thinks this location is a *gut* one. But of course he'll need to go over the bookkeeping thoroughly, as well as watch the customer traffic and investigate the inventory."

"*Ja*, of course. I'd be happy to go over all the books with him. When can he take over?" Esther bent to pick up the spilled paperwork.

Anna held up a hand. "Well, it's not a done deal yet. We're still in the talking stage, and there's always a chance it may fall through. He has a number of things he'll have to inspect first. But he sounds serious. We're having him over for supper tonight, so you'll have a chance to meet him. He did mention he wants you to continue managing the store, since you've done such a *gut* job."

A portion of Esther's elation drained away, though she hid that from her aunt. Managing the store was something she did as a labor of love to her aunt and uncle, but it was not what she wanted to continue doing forever. She had other hopes and dreams.

But all she said was, "*Ja*, sure, I'd be happy to continue managing." She dumped the bookkeeping items back on the desk. "And that means you and Uncle Paul can retire."

"*Ja*." Anna passed her hand over her face in a gesture of weariness. "The Lord is *gut*," she murmured.

Esther's heart went out to her. Her aunt had been in a lather of worry over her husband's health. Taking over the management of King's Mercantile in Chaffinch, Indiana, was the least Esther could do after her aunt and uncle had been her refuge in her time of need.

"Why don't you head home?" Esther suggested to her aunt. "I just have a bit more work to do, then I'll close up. It's been slow since that last tourist bus departed anyway."

"*Danke*." Anna smiled. "I'll have supper ready. The buyer will be at the *haus* at six o'clock, just so you know."

"I'll be home by then, don't worry."

After her aunt left, Esther finished her paperwork,

then closed the office door behind her. The store was quiet with that end-of-the-day feel. She watched as the employees went through the evening procedure of tidying shelves, sweeping floors and closing down their departments for the night. One or two lingering customers slowly made their way to the cash registers.

It was a familiar ritual, one Esther had performed nearly every day for seven years under her uncle's careful tutelage. When she started training, Esther herself had no idea she would have such a flair for numbers and management; but the happy result was she was able to lift much of the burden from her uncle's shoulders.

She glanced around at the spacious building, built in the mid-nineteenth century at the main crossroads of Chaffinch. If this mysterious businessman did indeed purchase the store, she hoped he wouldn't make things too modern-looking.

After saying goodbye to her employees, Esther recorded the day's receipts and wrote them in her ledger. Then she made sure the office space was tidy and welcoming. She didn't want to do anything that might jeopardize the man's interest in buying the store.

Afterward, she walked the half mile to her aunt and uncle's small farm, where she had lived for the past seven years. Aunt Anna had said the buyer knew her parents. That meant he must be familiar with Plum Grove, Indiana, where she'd grown up. Esther pressed a hand to her midsection, the familiar anxiety and feelings popping up at the thought of her hometown. Thankfully, it was all behind her.

As she approached the white clapboard King home—graceful as only turn-of-the-century buildings could be—Esther saw an unfamiliar horse hitched to the post, and a strange buggy by the barn. Smoothing down her apron and adjusting her *kapp*, Esther stepped inside the cheerful sage-and-cream farmhouse kitchen. Her greeting died on her lips.

It had been seven years, but she recognized him instantly.

It was Joseph Kemp.

Surely this couldn't be the man interested in buying the store? Esther's cheeks flared hot as she remembered the shameful humiliation of her teenage years, remembering the event that changed the course of her young life.

Joseph wore no beard, but his dark blue eyes and straight brown hair were just as she remembered. Laugh lines crinkled the corners of his mouth, and his skin was tanned from outdoor work. His straw hat had left an imprint on his hair.

The first thought that rocketed through her mind was flight. She glanced around for an escape route. But as he rose politely from his chair, she knew she had no choice but to brazen it out. She lifted her chin. *"Gut'n owed."*

"Esther Yoder, *ja*?"

"Ja."

"It's been a long time."

So much for the desperate wish that he wouldn't recognize her.

"Ja." She closed the door behind her and walked over to her uncle Paul and kissed him on the cheek.

Paul looked surprised. "You know each other?" he asked.

"I knew him in Plum Grove." Esther walked over to the kitchen sink, pumped the handle and washed her hands.

"That makes sense, since he knows your parents." Apparently oblivious to the tense overtone in the room, Aunt Anna stirred a pot on the stove. "And how is my brother and his wife?" she asked Joseph.

"They're doing well." Joseph talked with familiarity of the family Esther had left behind. His words caused her midsection to clench. There were times she desperately missed her family, since she saw them so rarely. But as for Plum Grove…no. She didn't miss it at all.

She puttered around the kitchen, avoiding Joseph's eyes. Instead she concentrated on wiping a counter, stirring a dish. Anything to keep from having to sit at the dinner table with the man.

"*Komm* and eat." Anna set a bowl on the table, and with reluctance, Esther stopped fussing around the kitchen and seated herself. When she bowed her head, she prayed for serenity.

She decided to ignore the past and concentrate on the present. Whatever messy history she had with Joseph, his purchase of the store was an answer to a prayer for her aunt and uncle. *Least said, soonest mended.* That was one of her aunt's favorite maxims, and this was a prime opportunity to test it.

"What makes you interested in our store for purchase?" She buttered a biscuit with a show of calm she didn't feel.

"A number of factors." Joseph took a bite of food and swallowed before answering. "This town is seeing a huge increase in the number of tourists, as you've no doubt noticed. The location is excellent, right at the crossroads. It's been in operation for a long time, suggesting stability. And everyone speaks highly of the

King family who has operated it for so long." He smiled at Paul.

"It's been a *gut* store," affirmed Paul. "But my sons aren't interested in running it. They trained in other fields and like what they're doing. If it hadn't been for Esther here, we probably would have sold it several years ago, after my health went downhill."

"Esther has been the manager for four years now," added Anna. "She's been training even longer. She knows the business better than anyone."

"Then you can be the one to show me the books and inventory," Joseph said to Esther.

"*Ja*, sure. It's tourist season, so we often have buses of visitors pass through. We'll have times we're very busy. But in the morning or late afternoon, when it's not so crowded, I can show you our inventory and our list of suppliers. And I'm sure you'll want to go over the books."

"Excellent. I have no doubt the store is in very *gut* hands, and assuming we proceed with the sale, I hope you'll continue managing it."

Esther murmured something noncommittal as her uncle took up the conversation. She didn't taste the food she put in her mouth. She was too busy choking on humiliation.

Joseph Kemp. Of all people to be buying the store!

Joseph watched Esther's skittish behavior throughout supper. It didn't surprise him when, as soon as the meal concluded, she offered to do dishes while her aunt and uncle urged him to relax in the parlor.

The years since they'd last seen each other had been difficult ones for him, dealing with Thomas, his unmanageable younger brother. And his sister Miriam, too—a young woman who desired nothing more than a chance to train in nursing. Ironically, Miriam had just gotten a job in Chaffinch's hospital, which had been part of his decision to consider the purchase of King's Mercantile here in the same town.

As for his brother Thomas—*Gott* help him, he never wanted to see Thomas again. Unfortunately his brother was a continual thorn in his side, with frequent scrapes with the law, outlandish behavior and the ability to cause shame to everyone.

The chaos of his earlier family life was in sharp contrast to the tranquility of the King and Yoder families, both here and in Plum Grove. Both families were upstanding, devout people. It was just Esther whose behavior had caused pain to her parents. He wasn't surprised when her teenaged escapades proved so embarrassing that she came to live with her aunt and uncle.

But, if her store management was any indication, it seems she'd settled down over the last few years.

And he had to admit, she'd grown up. Her dark blue eyes were steady and mature, her brown hair neatly tucked beneath her *kapp*. He knew she'd been baptized several years ago. No scandal or gossip touched her name. Unlike the town she'd left behind, here in Chaffinch, her reputation was unblemished.

He trailed Anna and Paul King into the parlor, filled with comfortable older furniture and items of domestic tranquility—a mending basket, a bookcase full of books, a newspaper.

"Please, take this chair." Paul gestured toward the most comfortable-looking seat.

"Esther?" called Anna from the parlor. "*Leibling*, would you make coffee for us?"

"*Ja*, sure," she responded from the kitchen.

Within a few minutes, Esther came out holding a tray with coffee cups, cream and sugar. Anna made sure his coffee was to his liking, but Joseph eyed Esther, who still seemed as nervous as a cat.

"My sister Miriam was asking about you the other day," he offered. "Do you remember her?"

"*Ja*, of course." Her face softened. "Miriam and I were best friends when we were younger. How is she?"

"It was disappointing when she left the church to become a nurse, but she loves her work."

He saw surprise in her face. "Miriam became a nurse!"

"*Ja*. She just got a job at the local hospital here in Chaffinch, so you'll probably see her soon."

"That would be *wunnerschee*. I've missed her." He heard a note of sadness in her voice. "She was always the nicest person…" Her voice trailed off.

Joseph picked up on her unspoken implication. "Unlike Thomas," he noted.

"*Ja*." Her voice was short. "Unlike Thomas."

"You know Joseph's family?" Anna asked in bewilderment.

"*Ja*." Esther looked at the floor for a moment. "I know his family. Aunt, if you don't need me, I've got some…some sewing to do."

"*Ja*, sure." Anna's face held a puzzled expression.

Esther then fled the room.

Joseph leaned back in his chair, a little embarrassed. He shouldn't have brought up the past. It was not his place to remind her of the scandal that had sent her fleeing Plum Grove. Instead, he was here to conduct business.

He would do well to remember that and keep his memories to himself.

Esther laid fabric pieces on the table in front of her, piecing together another quilt. Her eyes stung, and she forced the tears not to fall.

Was *Gott* playing a joke on her? The painful wound she'd buried seven years ago had healed over…or so she thought.

Now she realized it hadn't. It was just as raw as it ever was. Joseph, by his very presence, had reopened that wound.

She sniffed and wiped her eyes against the tears she couldn't hold back. The colorful patches of fabric, lit up by the evening sun pouring through her window, blurred.

When finished, the quilt she was working on would be sold in the store. Esther was pleased her sewing skills contributed in some way to the financial success of the emporium. Her aunt and uncle had taken her in seven years ago when she'd fled the scandal in Plum Grove. She wanted to help them in any way she could to thank them for taking her in when she needed it.

And now the store would be sold. Sold to the man whose behavior had ultimately sent her hundreds of miles away to another community. Very likely, it meant she had to work with him through the transition period. Oh yes, *Gott* had a sense of humor.

She thought about Miriam, Joseph's sister. A smile touched her lips as she recalled all the fun they'd had together as children, then later as teens. She and Miriam had been inseparable. Together they'd honed their sewing skills, producing beautiful quilts from a young age. Together they'd learned all the usual aspects of an Amish girlhood—milking cows, making butter, growing a garden, canning fruits and vegetables.

But it was sewing that became Esther's special province, an outlet for her creativity and a soothing pastime when she was troubled. Miriam, meanwhile, developed an interest in herbs and healing. It didn't surprise Esther in the least to hear her old friend had become a nurse, though it was a shame she'd had to leave the church to do so.

"Esther?"

She heard her aunt's footsteps coming down the uncarpeted hallway toward the sewing room. "In here, *aenti*." She hastily wiped her cheeks with a handkerchief, then stuffed it back in her pocket.

Anna poked her face in the doorway. "*Liebling*? Are you all right?"

"*Ja.*"

Her aunt scrutinized her for a few moments. "It sure doesn't seem that way. What's the matter?"

"Nothing."

"Lying is a sin, Esther, don't you know that?" With a gentle smile, Anna leaned against the doorframe. "You were quiet all through dinner, and then you didn't stay to talk with Joseph afterward, even though you're the one managing the store, and he'll need to know a lot of information only you can provide."

"I'm sorry if I was rude..."

"So you know Joseph?"

Esther's silence was answer enough. Anna came in

and sat down on the chair in front of the treadle sewing machine. "Tell me, child."

She sniffed and fished out her handkerchief again. "Well, if you must know, Joseph is the one who ruined my reputation when I was a teenager."

Anna, who knew the reason behind Esther's departure from Plum Grove, sucked in her breath. "*Ach*, Esther, I had no idea..."

"He's the one who spread gossip around the community. That's when you and Uncle Paul took me in so I could start my life over again."

"Come now, *liebling*, your life would have been fine if you'd stayed in Plum Grove, though we're grateful to *Gott* you came to live with us. But from what I know of this Joseph Kemp, it seems completely out of character for him to treat you that way."

"But I can assure you, he did. I will never, ever forget that."

"Or forgive?"

"*Ja*, maybe you're right. I haven't forgiven him." Esther fingered the quilt blocks in front of her. "I was just thinking it's a big joke on me to have Joseph be the one interested in buying the store. And I know how important it is to you to sell it. Uncle Paul will feel so much better if he no longer has to worry about it."

"We would consider it a gift from *Gott* if the store sold. And Joseph is the only one who's been serious about buying it."

"I know. I hoped when I took over as manager that Uncle Paul's health would improve since he was no longer involved in the day-to-day activities. But I know it's the money that worries him the most." Esther lifted her head and smoothed her features. "Don't worry, *aenti*. I won't say or do anything that would jeopardize Joseph's interest in purchasing the store. You can depend on me."

"Danke, liebling." Anna leaned down and kissed her cheek. "Selling the store would mean the world to your uncle."

Joseph guided his horse and buggy through the quiet side streets of Chaffinch toward the house where he was boarding with acquaintances. He didn't pay attention to the warm evening or the shady maple and oak trees that lined the sidewalk. Seeing Esther again after all these years had jump-started his memories of the past and his tumultuous relationship with his younger brother.

He had found Thomas and Esther in the barn that fateful day seven years ago. Somehow his brother had managed to sweet-talk Esther out of her clothes. It had truly been *Gott*'s hand that he'd gotten there before anything unseemly had happened. But his discovery of them had humiliated the young woman beyond anything. He wasn't surprised to hear that she had left town soon after to take up residence with her aunt and uncle. He wondered now why *Gott* had directed him to this particular town and this particular store. Was he meant to meet Esther again? It seemed so.

Esther was obviously a joy to her aunt and uncle and a solid reason why King's Mercantile was doing so well, especially in light of Paul King's increasing ill health.

If the sale became finalized, as he expected it would, he very much wanted Esther to continue managing the store.

And the only way that would happen, he knew, is if he never brought up the past.

Ever.

Chapter Two

Esther walked to the store the next morning, dreading the thought of spending the entire day with Joseph. She knew she had no choice, but that made no difference with her anxiety. It seemed she spent half the night sleepless, praying for serenity, reliving her scandalous past—a past that Joseph obviously remembered.

She sighed as she unlocked the store doors. She left them unlocked, as the other employees would be arriving shortly as well. At the very least, she wouldn't be alone with Joseph.

By the time Joseph stepped inside an hour later, the store was open for business and had a few early customers. He came inside quietly, like a customer, without fanfare. His dark hair was glossy in the morning sunshine. She smoothed down her apron and touched her *kapp* to make sure it wasn't askew.

"Guder mariye," she greeted him, her expression neutral. "What would you like to do first? I can give you a tour, show you the books, or anything you'd like."

"Guder mariye," he replied. "Let's start with a tour.

I'll be interested in seeing the store from an insider's perspective."

She nodded. She'd given tours before, so this was familiar territory.

Walking him through the various departments, she told him how each was dedicated to providing non-electric solutions, not just to the Plain People but also *Englischers* who simply preferred a simple approach to life.

The various departments included the area dedicated to selling wood-burning stoves, the lighting section full of oil lamps of every variety, the toy department featuring many Amish-made playthings for children, the book area that featured farming and homesteading reference materials. She showed him the laundry area featuring handmade soaps and clothes drying racks, the needle arts section which highlighted quilting, the kitchen area with endless food preservation equipment and supplies, and the tool section with hand tools, both large and small.

"We're always looking for new products to add," she told him as they lingered in the tool section. "We've just started carrying beekeeping equipment." She gestured toward zippered veils and beehive boxes. "Interest in beekeeping is growing, and enough customers requested certain products that we knew it would be wise to start carrying them."

"Smart." Joseph nodded, then watched as an older man examined a selection of wood-splitting tools. "And you have something for every age group."

"*Ja.* The toy section is especially busy over the Christmas holidays, as you can imagine."

"How many of your vendors are Amish?"

"At least half. When my uncle opened the store thirty years ago, his intention was to pull together in one location many of the products Amish people wanted and needed. But about fifteen years ago, it was discovered by the wider world when we had some news coverage. Things kind of exploded as we became a tourist destination and even an educational facility as people clamored to learn how to can food or how to do laundry by hand. Now, we've become a source of income for many of the regional Plain People, who provide us with everything from hats to tools to clothing to toys. Our best-selling line of wood cookstoves, for example, is made by an Amish family business in Ohio."

"That's *gut*. I like the idea of providing outlets for products made by the local Amish communities."

"*Ja*, it's been an honor to work here."

"I'm glad you'll be continuing." said Joseph.

She met his eyes. *"Ja,"* she said blandly.

It wasn't a lie, exactly. She would remain manager—at least until the sale was completed.

He turned toward the center of the store where the cash registers were located. "How many people do you currently employ?"

"Twenty here in the store. We also have the warehouse about a block away, where we have another five people. They handle incoming inventory and fill mail orders."

"And you manage all the employees as well as the inventory and shipping?"

"Ja."

"And you're, what, twenty-four? That's a lot of responsibility for someone your age."

She bristled, then remembered to keep calm. Mature store managers didn't bristle, after all. "Keep in mind

I've been in training for this position for seven years, ever since leaving Plum Grove. My uncle's health began declining shortly after I started working here, so he and Aunt Anna began training me for management, especially since I showed an aptitude for it. I love this store."

"It shows." Just then, a tour bus arrived, and the store began to get busy. "Do this many *Englisch* have an interest in canning jars and gardening tools?" he asked with a twinkle in his eyes.

"A surprising number," she replied, catching the humor. "But most just come to glimpse the simpler side of life. That said, we actually dedicate a lot of our efforts to education. So many people want to know how to can vegetables or grow a garden in their backyard or sew on a treadle machine or hang laundry on a clothesline. Our employees do their best to answer questions and teach them how to do things the old-fashioned way. We also bring in speakers or put on teaching seminars, especially during summer months when visitors are at their peak."

"What kind of seminars?"

"We've had quilting seminars, canning classes, gardening demonstrations, that kind of thing. We've also had guest speakers coming in from out of the area, especially experts in some aspect of sustainable living."

"Admirable."

"Thank you." She started to smooth down her apron until she realized it was becoming a nervous habit, so she kept her hands still. It pleased her that Joseph seemed determined to keep things on a professional level. He made no reference to her former life, certainly not to the gossip that ruined her reputation and her chance at marriage. "The educational aspect is actually fairly recent, but it's been a terrific success. Most of the people wanting to learn things are *Englischer*, and it's nice to see so much interest in domestic and rural interests."

"Such as that?" He indicated one of her older employees, who was explaining something on a sheet of paper to a young mother, then gesturing toward canning supplies.

"*Ja.* My guess is the customer is just learning how to can. Seems like she's being given some instructions on easy canning projects."

Joseph stood quiet for a few moments, watching the exchange. The young woman smiled and loaded a large pot and a dozen canning jars into her cart and tucked the instruction sheet in as well.

"You're right," he said. "Nice job by the employee."

"Her name is Rhonda. She's worked here for years, ever since her last child got married. She's an expert canner."

"And it shows me the level of customer service you offer. I like to see that."

"*Danke.* Most of our employees have been here for a long time. They're good at what they do."

"And you're clearly good at managing them."

Surprised by his praise, she gave him a nod. Beyond gratitude for his professional interest in the store, she knew she had to be polite to the man, for the sake of her uncle.

"Another possibility is to do some rearrangement in the store." Joseph, apparently oblivious to her internal turmoil, pivoted in a slow circle, taking in the various different departments. "For example, a sort of play area to keep children safe while their parents shop."

"Ja." Esther raised her eyebrows. "I hadn't thought of that. It's a *gut* idea, and I think I can suggest a space for it."

"This store has a tremendous amount of potential."

She tried to keep the eagerness from her voice. "Does this mean you've decided to buy it?"

"Not yet. I need to look over the books, the inventory, insurance rates, that kind of thing."

"I have it all ready. Just let me know when it's convenient for you."

"Probably tomorrow. I'll plan on setting aside the whole day for it. If you provide me with the documentation I need, I shouldn't have to bother you too much."

"You can work in my office. It's in that back corner." She pointed. "Tomorrow is fine. I'm usually busy on the floor on Wednesdays anyway, since that's the day most of the new stock comes in, so we're all busy filling shelves."

"Then don't be surprised if I spend some of my time watching the process."

"Ja, sure. You'll probably need a break from pouring over the books anyway."

"Danke." He smiled at her.

For the briefest moment, Esther smiled back. She was used to smiling at customers, a sort of automatic response. But Joseph was different. A smile implied a friendship she wasn't ready—or willing—to accept.

Instead she turned away from him. "Where are you staying, by the way?"

"With some acquaintances out on Turner Road."

"The Herschberger family?"

"Ja, Matthew and Sarah Herschberger."

"They are fine people. They can fill you in on some of the details of the town as well."

"What are your plans for the rest of the day?" he asked. "In other words, what would you normally do if I wasn't here?"

"Mostly just walking the floor, helping customers, ringing up sales, that kind of thing."

"Will it trouble you if I just wander around and observe?"

"Of course not. If you'd like to sit near the cash register, I can fetch a stool or a chair. There's coffee and tea in back. Make yourself at home."

"*Danke.* I will."

Esther moved away to ring up a sale for a customer, aware she was being observed. The woman tourist chattered about the beauty of the countryside and the charm of the old-fashioned store. Esther had heard such remarks a thousand times, but she smiled and agreed and thanked the lady.

She walked the floor, asking customers if they had any questions or needed any assistance. She endured the usual questions about her *kapp* and modest attire. She watched some children squeal over the toy section and realized Joseph's suggestion for a play area was a good one.

And she also thought about Joseph—what he had done since she'd last seen him as a teenager. Obviously he had done well financially, since he already owned two stores. Where had he learned his business acumen? A well-to-do Amish man was something of an anomaly, and she realized it made her wary.

With a pneumatic sigh, another tour bus pulled up into the store's parking lot, and Esther braced herself for another influx of tourists. They were the lifeblood of the store, even if they got annoying sometimes.

Out of the corner of his eye, Joseph watched Esther at work. He was impressed. He knew good management when he saw it.

Esther's approach with customers and staff alike was calm, patient and kindly. He watched her interactions with employees and picked up nothing but respect and affection. This was a mark in favor of finalizing his purchase of the store—excellent management already in place.

He prowled among the store's departments, eavesdropping on customer conversations, watching the purchasing patterns, noting which displays attracted the most attention.

"Look at the details. This is handmade, no question about it."

He glanced over to see two middle-aged *Englisch* women talking to each other, deep in admiration over a quilt. He sidled over to listen.

"I don't think I've ever seen a quilt pattern made to look like a puzzle," said the second woman. She examined a tag. "The price is right for a handmade quilt, and it would fit our bed. I think I'll get this one." She lifted the quilt from its display stand.

"I'm tempted by that one." The first woman pointed. "The colors are lovely. Oooh look, Barbara. You can get a customized quilt."

"Really? Let me see." Barbara seized a piece of paper, scanned it, then looked at the quilt in her arms. She shook her head. "No, I like this one. I'm going to get it."

The women moved off. Curious, Joseph stepped into the quilting section and examined the inventory with a closer eye.

The women were right. The quilts were clever, among the nicest he'd ever seen—and he'd seen a lot. Some of the quilts were traditional designs of typical Amish patterns—double wedding ring, log cabin, nine-patch—but quite a number were a unique style made to look like interlocked puzzle pieces. He examined one quilt with a knowledgeable air. Machine-stitched but with just enough idiosyncrasies to recognize it was made with a treadle sewing machine.

And the tourist was correct—the price was right. He examined a second quilt, then a third, noting the pleasing color combinations and generous sizes. The maker of these quilts was an artist, no question about it.

He examined the tag on one of the quilts and learned they were made by none other than Esther Yoder.

Amazing. Whatever awkward teenage girl he remembered back in Plum Grove, Esther had clearly matured into a talented, artistic businesswoman.

A third tourist bus pulled in, then a fourth, and the store became crowded with customers. Esther hardly seemed to have a chance to leave the cash register. He watched as she answered questions and fielded comments with amazing patience. She even managed to deftly avoid some flirtatious remarks directed her way by some of the bolder *Englisch* men.

At last, toward late afternoon, things slowed down enough that she was able to collapse on a stool behind the register counter.

He sauntered over. "Whew. That was a busy stretch."

"*Ja*, tell me about it." She shrugged. "But it's not

unusual this time of year. You can see why it was too much for Uncle Paul to handle."

"You handle it well."

She eyed him with a suspicious air, he thought. *"Danke."*

"And I see you're the one behind many of those quilts." He gestured toward the area where the quilts were displayed.

To his surprise, her features softened. *"Ja."* She smiled, the first genuine smile he'd seen out of her. "I enjoy making them."

"When do you find the time?"

"Evenings. Sometimes early mornings." She looked down at the floor and muttered, "They help me forget the past."

He ignored the remark. "Did you design them yourself?"

"Ja." She raised her head, and he was pleased to see her smile back. "I learned to quilt from *Mamm*, of course, but I fine-tuned my skills with Aunt Anna. She's an expert quilter."

"How do you choose your colors? What are your favorite color combinations?"

She drew in her brows. "Those are unusual questions coming from a man. Usually it's just the women who want to know."

"I own two other stores, and quilts are a huge part of the appeal in Amish-owned mercantiles. I've learned a lot about them as a result."

She nodded. "I became enamored of the puzzle styles many years ago and choose to concentrate on them. So many other women are talented in quilting, but not many others make puzzle quilts."

"You have several types of color themes, but they all seem to focus on earthy colors."

"*Ja.* I tend to prefer muted greens, browns, beiges, reds—as you say, earth tones." Her voice grew more animated. "I love making quilts—it's fun and relaxing for me."

"How many other suppliers do you have for quilts? And are they all Amish?"

"*Ja.* We have about five women who make them for us. They're all older, with their children grown." She cocked her head. "Do you plan to expand the quilt display area?"

"I'm thinking about it. I was watching the interest from various customers throughout the day. The quilts are beautiful and eye-catching, and I think placing them closer to the front door would be an improvement."

She paused for a moment, as if considering his suggestion, then said, "*Ja*, I think you're right."

He was pleased she didn't seem hostile to the idea. Of course, he knew she was not in a position to oppose him since she wanted to secure his agreement to purchase her uncle's store. But still, he found her cooperation pleasant.

He nodded. "I think we're going to get along just fine, Esther."

He saw her stiffen and was sorry to see the glow of enthusiasm leave her eyes. She didn't respond right away to his comment but instead turned to rearrange some items near the cash register.

"As long as it helps Uncle Paul and Aunt Anna," she muttered.

"You think a lot of them, don't you?"

She stopped fidgeting and met his eyes. "They took me in when I needed refuge. I love them as much as I love my parents."

"I can understand why. If you don't mind my asking, what are your uncle's health issues? Running this store is a lot of work, but it seems a shame he has to sell after so many years."

"He has high blood pressure. It's slowing him down."

Joseph frowned. "Has he been to see a doctor? High blood pressure is one of the easiest conditions to control."

"I know." Esther passed a hand over her face. "But he's like many men. He won't admit he has a problem."

"He's admitted it enough that he's looking to sell the store, *ja*?"

"*Ja*, true. Really, he just wants to retire, and who can blame him? He's worked so hard all his life."

"And now I'm the one coming to the rescue." He quirked a grin at her.

She didn't smile back. "I won't deny I hope that's the case. It would help him a tremendous amount knowing he's no longer responsible for it, even though most of the day-to-day operations fall on me. And to an extent, Aunt Anna."

"Well, I like what I've seen so far. The store has a tremendous amount of potential, and it's better organized than either of the other two stores I own."

"Tomorrow you can spend the day looking over the books and inventory lists and anything else you need. I'll help however I can." She smoothed down her apron, then looked him full in the face. "My goal is to convince you this store is worth purchasing."

"Then we see eye to eye." For some reason, he couldn't help himself. "All forgiven?" he asked.

A hard expression came over her. It was clear she knew exactly what he meant.

"No," she said low. "It's not."

Chapter Three

"So how did it go at the store today?" Aunt Anna asked as she spooned macaroni from a pot on the stove into a large bowl.

"It actually went better than I expected." Esther gave her uncle a peck on the cheek and went to wash her hands at the kitchen sink. "He spent the day following my every move, but that's to be expected. He looked into every nook and cranny, eavesdropped on conversations with customers, watched the staff work, and made a few suggestions for rearranging the store."

"What was his overall impression?" asked Uncle Paul.

Esther heard the eagerness in his voice. "Very favorable," she assured him, "though he still hasn't committed himself yet to purchasing. But he very much liked the history of the place, how you brought in that old barn and reassembled it to expand the store, that kind of thing. He had nothing but praise for how you organized everything."

"Did he see the warehouse?"

"Not yet. I intend to show him that tomorrow, espe-

cially since we'll have some of the local vendors dropping off their merchandise."

"Did he say anything about your management?"

"He seemed to think I'd done a *gut* job. I told him
I'd be interested in continuing to manage it if he buys
the store."

"Did he, ah, bring up anything personal?" Anna inquired as she brought the food to the table.

"No. And for that, I'll grudgingly give him credit."
Esther seated herself. She paused for the silent blessing,
then continued, "I think at some level he understands
if we're going to work together, he can't dredge up any
painful memories from the past."

"And you—how do you feel about it?"

"I'm not sure," she admitted. "I appreciate that he's
keeping things strictly on a professional level. But every
time I see him, it reminds me of what happened." She
relaxed her hand which she realized had been clenching her fork. She shrugged with what she hoped was
nonchalance. "We'll make it work."

"I know this is hard on you, *liebling*." Her uncle patted her hand before buttering a biscuit. "But my prayer
is he buys the store, even if it means you'll have to
work with him."

"*Ach,* Uncle Paul, I know that." Esther smiled at him.
"And I told Aunt Anna last night, I promise not to do
anything that would jeopardize him buying the place."

"That's *gut*, then." Anna spooned some casserole on
her plate and turned the conversation to other matters.

By the next morning, Esther had worked things out
in her mind to keep things between her and Joseph
strictly professional. She was used to working with the

public, which sometimes meant cantankerous customers or difficult complaints. She could handle working with Joseph Kemp, whatever their previous history.

In that frame of mind, she unlocked the store doors and welcomed the employees as they filed in. With no customers yet, she was able to set up the complimentary coffee and tea area, walk around the departments to make sure nothing was amiss and discuss with two of her senior staff some possible demonstrations they would host in the next few months. She also assembled the materials Joseph would need to review the store's fiscal history.

Joseph breezed in just as the first tour bus of the day off-loaded its passengers.

"Guder mariye," she greeted him. "Since things are getting busy, I can set you up in my office to start looking over the books."

He glanced around at the throngs of customers. "Let's do that."

"Follow me." She left her post at the cash register after summoning another employee to take over.

The back office was a peaceful, quiet oasis. Esther had furnished it with an old wooden desk, several antique oak file cabinets left over from the days when her uncle managed the store and a secondhand oak chair that squeaked as it rolled around on its wheels. The screened window was raised, allowing a gentle summer breeze to waft around the room.

"As you can see, I've gathered everything you should need." She pointed to various documents. "I keep everything by hand, of course, but it's all accurate and up to date." She indicated various piles of papers. "Here is our collection of suppliers, this is our current and past inventory, here are details of our insurance coverage, and of course, these ledger books record our income and expenses. Receipts are here. Sales slips are there. Anything else you might need, just let me know."

"You do everything by hand?" he inquired in some surprise. "Nothing on a computer?"

"No, of course not." She frowned, wondering if this aspect of her bookkeeping was an insurmountable drawback. "I've never used a computer."

"It's a big job, keeping track of a store this size solely by hand."

"I'm *gut* with numbers." Her voice was cool. "And you know as well as I do that using computers is discouraged in our faith."

"True, but there are exceptions. This might need to be one of them." He grinned at her. "To be honest, I'm not all that familiar with computers either. The solution might be to hire someone who is."

"I've thought about that too," Esther admitted. "Right now we don't have a catalog or online sales, for example. We get—or used to get—a fair bit of business with mail-in orders through the catalog, but as the internet gained popularity, mail orders dropped off. I keep thinking of all the sales opportunities we're missing."

"*Ja.* That's almost a whole separate business." His eyes gleamed. "It might be worth hiring a specialist to help the store build a website and develop online sales."

Esther frowned. "Won't that go against the *Ordnung*?"

He shook his head. "I don't know the bishop of your church here, but if you remember the bishop in Plum Grove, he understood sometimes technology is needed to keep our businesses running. It does no good if we can't compete with the *Englisch* and we lose our livelihood."

"*Ja*, true." She shook her head. "It's too much for me to think about. I'm busy enough as it is, and I know nothing about how any of that works."

"Well, it's worth considering for sure and certain." He cocked his head toward the main floor of the building. "Sounds like another busload of tourists has arrived."

"I think you're right." Esther hoped her handwritten bookkeeping materials and lack of internet presence would not deter Joseph from making a decision about the financial viability of the store. "Also, we have some vendors who will be dropping off inventory this afternoon by the warehouse. If you want, you can monitor how it's done. Or even pitch in."

"I'd like that." He seated himself in the squeaky desk chair.

She smoothed down her apron. "Now, if you'll excuse me, I need to get back to work."

"May I take you to lunch later on?"

Esther paused, startled. It was the first personal remark he'd made. "I—"

"Purely as a business meal, of course," he said. "You *do* eat lunch, don't you?"

"*Ja*, but mostly at my desk."

"I noticed there's a restaurant just around the corner. It would be my pleasure to take you to lunch."

"*Danke,*" she replied weakly. "That would be nice."

"*Gut.*" He nodded toward the door. "I'll be in here looking over the books. Let me know when it's convenient for you to take lunch."

"*Ja.*" She turned and fled.

Stopping at the threshold to the store's main floor, hand on her chest, she wondered why a simple business invitation to lunch should throw her off-kilter like this. She was so busy focusing on her professional responsibilities that she hadn't prepared herself for the one-on-one interaction with him.

She waded out among the happy customers, listening to chatter about the products on display. She answered questions and assisted in sales. And through it all, she thought about having lunch with Joseph.

A bit past one o'clock, she turned and saw Joseph standing near the cash register, seemingly looking over a display of books, but in reality, she knew, watching the ebb and flow of customers. After the past few hours of assisting patrons and addressing inquiries, she felt more equal to the task of having lunch with him.

She laughed to herself. Here she was, making a mountain out of a molehill over a simple business lunch. It's not like he was courting her or anything. She twitched her apron straight and walked toward him.

"Did you find everything satisfactory? Any discrepancies?" she asked.

"*Nein*. You've done an excellent job of keeping everything in detail." He stroked his beardless chin. "Are you hungry? It's a bit late, but I figure it was better to wait until the lunch crowd thinned out."

"*Ja*, I'm hungry. Let me tell the assistant manager I'll be gone. Give me a moment."

Ten minutes later, she found herself seated across a small table in a quiet corner of a nearby restaurant.

Joseph waited until the waitress had taken their orders. Then he leaned back in his chair and smiled at her. "I've decided to go through with the purchase of the store."

Elation flooded through Esther and she grinned. But she refrained from pumping a fist in the air. "*Danke!* This will mean the world to Uncle Paul."

He chuckled. "I'm quite pleased too. I hadn't realized until I saw the store for myself how busy it is, how well respected and solid. In some ways, it's the best investment I've ever seen."

"I can't wait to tell my aunt and uncle when I get home tonight."

"Perhaps we should go together. They won't be expecting me for supper, but hopefully that won't be a problem."

"No, not at all." All sour feelings toward the man evaporated in the happy moment. Her uncle would be able to rest, regain his strength and concentrate on puttering in his garden as he loved to do. She smiled dreamily. "What a difference this will make to Uncle Paul."

"How often does your uncle come into the store?"

"Only about once a month now. I think *aenti* tries to keep him from coming any more than he has to. He used to live and breathe the store, but now I can see the stress on his face whenever he comes through the doors."

"Then hopefully this will help to keep his blood pressure under control."

"*Ja.*"

The waitress delivered their food, and after a silent blessing, she tucked in.

"There are some changes I'd like to discuss with you after the sale goes through," Joseph continued, buttering a roll. "I think they'll be improvements for both flow patterns for customers, as well as offer some different incentives."

"What kind of changes?" Some of her elation drained away. "I hope you don't think my management has been subpar?"

"Not at all. Just the opposite, in fact. Your management is what convinced me the store is a good business deal. That doesn't mean there isn't room for improvement, of course."

She felt mollified. "You mentioned a child's play area, which I think is an excellent idea. What else did you have in mind?"

"Expanding the quilting section," he replied. "Yesterday I watched how many people, especially *Englisch* women, lingered in that area. I think we could double the space devoted to quilts, while shifting over and tightening up other areas without compromising display spaces."

His emphasis on quilts gave her pause. One of her dearest dreams was opening a quilt store of her own. But if Joseph expanded the quilting section of King's Mercantile, it might result in too much competition to make her own dream a success.

She shoved away the thought. Right now, she couldn't do anything that might encourage Joseph to change his mind. Instead, she nodded and said, "*Ja*, I think that would work…"

"And the whole store will have to be computerized. As we discussed earlier, we would need to develop an online presence. That's how people shop these days. Plus, it would widen our potential customer base dramatically…"

By the end of the meal, Esther was quite pleased with

herself. No hint of her past rose up to mar the professionalism of the lunch. She walked beside Joseph as they headed back toward the store.

"Do you have more to review with the bookkeeping materials?" she asked. She nodded thanks when he opened the door for her.

"No, not for now. I would rather watch the customers and mentally address the layout."

Esther paused, watching through a window as yet another tourist bus turned the corner into the parking lot. "Looks like you'll get your wish," she said dryly. "Brace yourself."

"Does the volume of *Englischer* visitors bother you?"

"It did when I first started working in the store. But now I'm used to it. Most of them are lovely people, of course, and I commend that they're trying to find products and ideas for living a more sustainable lifestyle. Like that young mother we saw yesterday, embarking on her first canning project. That's the kind of customer that keeps me going."

"But…?"

She caught the hint of humor in his eyes. "But some others can be a challenge," she admitted. "I imagine that's the bane of every retail establishment—the occasional customer we want nothing more than to push out the door."

She and Joseph moved to one side as the store's front door opened and a veritable deluge of people poured in, talking in loud voices and gesticulating.

"Excuse me, please," she told him. "I'd better get back to work."

Esther let the assistant manager know she was back

on the floor, and for the next two hours, she was busy ringing up sales and answering questions.

"Are you Amish?"

She turned and saw an *Englisch* man in his thirties. He eyed her *kapp*.

"Ja," she replied. "May I help you?"

He moved closer. "I like a woman who looks old-fashioned. What do you say we go get a cup of coffee?"

"Why?" She smiled sweetly.

"So I can get to know you better."

"Why?"

"Er, um, well…"

"Sir, I'm the manager of this store. I'm afraid I don't have time for coffee."

"Oooh, a smart businesswoman to boot." He gave her a smarmy smile and laid a hand on her arm. "Now I definitely want to get to know you better."

She brushed his hand off and moved away, keeping the saccharine smile plastered on her face. "You know, a very wise man once said if anyone looks at a woman in the wrong way, he has already committed adultery with her in his heart."

The man looked annoyed. "Is that what you think I'm doing?"

She looked directly into his eyes. *"Ja."*

"Oh." He dropped his own gaze to the floor and fiddled with a ring on his left hand. "Can't blame me for trying," he muttered. Shrugging, he stalked away.

Esther turned and caught Joseph's eye. He lifted a single eyebrow in amusement and approached her.

"Does that happen a lot?" he asked.

"More often than you'd think. I just consider it an

occupational hazard. Some men look at a *kapp* as a challenge."

"I was about to come rescue you until I realized you didn't need the help."

"I keep a list of Bible verses on hand for just such an occasion."

"And it worked. How often does this sort of thing happen?"

"Perhaps once a month." She gestured around the store. "As I mentioned earlier, 99.9 percent of people who come through the doors are lovely. But once in a while, we get a bad apple."

He chuckled. "Nice job. You handled it well."

"I've had practice," she muttered.

Joseph found himself more impressed with Esther than he anticipated. Her adept handling of the obnoxious male customer—countering the man's advances with a Bible verse!—increased his respect. He wondered if her strength of character was despite or because of what happened when she was a teenager. Either way, he found the coincidence of connecting with her after all these years an intriguing one.

The afternoon was busy. He strolled through the store, making mental notes about altering the layout, when he saw her threading her way among customers and merchandise. "Some of the local vendors are starting to arrive to deliver their merchandise," she told him. "If you want, you can come see the warehouse, meet the manager and some of the vendors too."

"*Ja*, I'd like that."

"Follow me. We'll go out the back door."

He trailed her through a discreet door behind a display into the bright June sunshine and fell in next to her on the sidewalk.

"The warehouse is about a block away." She pointed to a building. "It's not on the main street, but it's convenient and close. Vendors usually arrive on Wednesday afternoons to deliver their merchandise."

"These are local vendors, I assume?"

"*Ja*, mostly Plain People. Amish and Mennonite. Some arrive with horse and wagon, some by car. More distant vendors ship their merchandise, and it arrives at different times, but Wednesday afternoon is the only day we accept merchandise in person."

"How do you log in the merchandise?"

"We have preprinted forms. They're at the warehouse. We log in each shipment as it arrives. Tomorrow I'll do paperwork, and then we start restocking the shelves. Often we stay late for that."

"I'll help, then. I want to learn your process."

She turned, and he saw a look of surprise on her face. "*Ja, danke.* Usually, I'm by myself."

"You stock the store by yourself?" He frowned. It seemed far too big a task for one person.

"No, of course not." She resumed walking. "There are three or four others who help stock the store after-hours on Thursdays. But I log in the entire inventory by myself."

"And you've been able to keep up without using a computer?"

"*Ja.* As I said before, I've never used a computer, so I wouldn't know where to start even if I had one. But we've streamlined the process over the years, and I do fine by hand."

Privately, Joseph thought she was foolish to persist

in hand tallies for a store of this size and complexity. Computerizing the inventory and bookkeeping was one of the first things he planned to do. He didn't think it would be hard to hire someone with the necessary qualifications.

They turned the corner behind the warehouse building, and Joseph saw several vendors already in the parking lot unloading their products. A store employee stood by with a clipboard and pen. People trundled hand trucks and trolley carts back and forth.

"*Guder nammidaag*, Charles." Esther greeted the young man.

Charles looked up. "*Guder nammidaag.* You're just in time. Things are getting busy."

"Charles, this is Joseph Kemp. He's the man who will be buying the store. Joseph, Charles is our warehouse manager."

Charles broke into a huge grin and reached out to shake hands. "Nice to meet you! I'm so glad to hear it will sell. What a relief for Paul and Anna."

Joseph noted the twinkle in the man's eyes and lack of beard under the Amish hat. "Nice to meet you too. I'm pleased by what I've seen so far."

"We'd better get busy logging in inventory," said Esther, interrupting. "It looks like more people are arriving." She walked through the open metal roll-up door of the warehouse. Just inside, she pulled two additional clipboards hanging from nails in the wall. She handed one of them to Joseph.

Joseph was pleased to see the system ran smoothly, and he realized Esther was right: the process was streamlined and efficient…or as efficient as it could be without a computer.

"This is very well done," he told her. "I'm pleased to be the buyer of this facility. I think it will be an easy business to maintain, especially—" he looked over where Esther stood, a clipboard still in her hands "—if you continue as manager."

She paused, then gave him a neutral smile. "I'm pleased you're putting this much trust in me. Especially after…" She stopped speaking.

Instinctively, Joseph knew that she'd almost referenced the scandal that had sent her fleeing her hometown as a teen.

Whatever had happened in the past, she had certainly become a respected member of the community here in Chaffinch. "I won't ever dredge up the past," he assured her.

Hot color flowed into her cheeks and she looked at the floor. *"Danke,"* she said in a low voice. "I don't know why you of all people should be the one to buy the store, but I'm grateful for my aunt and uncle's sake."

"I'll never give you reason to regret anything," he assured her.

To his surprise, she raised her head, and a gleam of hostility shone in her eyes. "I'm not the one who has things to regret," she snapped. "If anyone behaved shamefully, it wasn't me." She whirled around. "I need to get back to the store. I'm sure you have other things you want to look over in the warehouse before it closes. Take your time." She trotted away, almost running in her haste.

Joseph was so startled that he stared after her. Now what did she mean by that comment? He's the one who caught *her* seven years ago in that compromising situation. How could she claim it wasn't shameful?

Yet, he knew the aftermath of the incident spread far and fast, ruining her reputation to the point where she'd escaped Plum Grove. He blamed his brother Thomas for that.

Yet something was amiss here. He shook his head, recalling his brother's involvement and Esther's behavior. Was his memory faulty? He didn't think so, but then again, seven years was no small stretch of time.

There was a mystery here, and he intended to get to the bottom of it.

Chapter Four

"I'll walk back with you to your aunt and uncle's."

Esther looked up from her task of cashing out the register. Joseph finished making notations on a pad of paper. The store was quiet and all the employees had gone home. The last tour bus had departed an hour ago.

"If you want." She returned to her counting. "I'll be about another fifteen minutes."

He nodded and walked off. She was grateful he didn't talk about her blunder in the warehouse during the afternoon. She'd been kicking herself for allowing a glimpse of truth to seep through a crack in the defenses she'd built around herself. Seven years was a long time to seal away a painful wound, and it surprised her how easily that crack had appeared.

She finished tallying numbers from the day's sales and recorded them in a ledger, which she placed on the desk in her office. Then she tucked the money from the day's receipts in a zippered pouch in the safe. Closing and locking her office window, she then proceeded to close down the rest of the store.

"Have you ever had a break-in?" Joseph inquired, trailing along as she went through the end-of-day routine.

"Just once, above five years ago. Someone broke a window and stole some merchandise, but not much. We ended up retrofitting all the glass windows with security film, which strengthens the glass. It's not a perfect solution, but we're also not much of a target for thieves." A ghost of a smile turned up the corners of her mouth. "Not many burglars are interested in looting canning jars or butter churns."

He chuckled. "*Ja*, I see your point."

Within a few minutes, her nightly routine was complete, and she braced herself for the half-mile walk to her aunt and uncle's house alone with Joseph.

She was inclined to stay silent, but Joseph was chatty. "It seems you've become quite a success since I've last seen you," he remarked.

"*Danke.*" Unwilling to dwell on her own past, she neatly turned the tables. "But what about you? All I know is you own two other stores in other towns, and now you're buying Uncle Paul's mercantile. You've obviously had a successful career."

"*Ja.* Did you know I left the Amish for a few years?"

Startled, she stared at him. "No! I had no idea."

"I wanted to go to college and study business. But I soon learned that about half of all classes needed for a degree don't involve the subject you're studying, so I took a more unorthodox approach. I just took the classes I thought I'd need, then apprenticed in an Amish store in Ohio. I learned what I needed to learn, then I came home and was baptized."

"Why were you so determined to learn business?"

"I don't know." His gaze lingered on the fields and

farms that crowded the edge of the town. "All I know is *Gott* gave me a desire to run mercantile businesses. I've always been fascinated with how it all operates. The first store I bought was a small run-down place in a little town in Indiana. I was able to turn it around within a year. It's turning a profit now. Pretty much the same story for the second business I bought. Then I heard about your uncle's interest in selling his store from your parents. It's by far the best-run store I've seen. It's more expensive to buy, obviously, but a lot less work in the long run since it's already turning a profit."

"Do you intend to keep buying stores?" she inquired. "Three seems like a lot."

"I might sell the other two," he admitted, "and focus just on this one. I'm not in business to become rich. That's not the Amish way. I'm in business because I like being in business. I like businesses that help others, and that's why I like the model your store uses—educating the customer, offering classes and workshops, having trained employees."

"*Ja*, that's Uncle Paul's philosophy," she replied. "All those buses that come through can get to be a bit much. But for every gawking busload of tourists, there are a handful of people who genuinely want to learn some aspect of a do-it-yourself lifestyle."

"Like that young mother who wanted to learn how to can food, the one your employee was helping earlier."

"*Ja*. Exactly."

With a start, Esther realized just how much Joseph had changed since their teenage years. He was now a level-headed, responsible businessman. Did he regret the hurtful gossip he spread about her seven years before? Did he feel remorse for his part of ruining her young reputation?

Because the Joseph now walking by her side was a far, far different person than the one she'd left behind in her hometown. If she wasn't careful, her respect for his professional accomplishments might turn to admiration. And frankly, that was the last thing she wanted.

Her home, the one she shared with her aunt and uncle, loomed ahead. She saw her uncle hunched over in the garden. "See Uncle Paul? As he's gotten older, that's what gives him the most pleasure. Working in the garden. He's a whiz at growing vegetables. I think he's just gotten tired of running the store even after all the years of hard work he put into building it. He'll be so happy to learn you've decided to buy it."

"He mentioned to me that none of his children want to run it. I find that hard to believe."

"They all chose different paths—farming, carpentry, construction. I think that's why they were so happy when I took to managing the store." She shrugged. "*Gott* gave me the gift of management, it seems. Even better, I enjoy it."

As they approached the house, Uncle Paul straightened up from rows of tomatoes and saw them. He lifted an arm in greeting.

"I hope your aunt doesn't mind an unexpected guest for dinner," commented Joseph.

"I'm sure she won't, especially after you tell them both your news." Esther climbed the side porch steps and pushed open the kitchen door. "Aunt Anna? I've brought Joseph Kemp for dinner. Is that *oll recht*?"

"*Ja*, sure." Anna turned from the stove. "*Gut'n owed*, Joseph."

"Gut'n owed." He sniffed the air. "Whatever you're cooking smells wonderful."

Paul entered the kitchen, and Esther immediately went to peck him on the cheek. "Sorry to bring an unexpected guest," she commented.

"We always have room." Paul smiled at Joseph. "Wash up and sit down!"

"Ja, dinner is just about ready," said Anna.

Within moments, the food was on the table. Heads bowed for the silent blessing.

"How did everything go in the store today?" inquired Paul. He hefted the bowl of casserole to Joseph so he could serve himself first.

"It went well," replied Esther. She found herself full of excitement at the good news Joseph hadn't yet revealed. "Busy. Joseph spent the morning looking over the books, then in the afternoon, he saw the warehouse and the week's inventory coming in from the local vendors."

"And did you like what you saw?" Paul asked Joseph.

"Ja." He paused for drama. "So much so that I've made the decision to purchase the store."

For a moment, startled silence greeted his words. Then Anna cried out and clasped her hands, and Paul cheered, then clapped Joseph on the back.

"That's wonderful! That's wonderful!" Anna's eyes welled up.

"The Lord is *gut*!" exclaimed Paul. "What a relief!"

"I *told* you they'd be happy," said Esther with a grin.

Joseph laughed. "I'm pleased to be the bearer of such good news."

When the hoopla died down, Uncle Paul took a bite

of his casserole, grinning throughout. "What made you decide?" he inquired.

"A number of things, not least of which is the approach you've taken with the store. I like the emphasis on education and demonstrations. I have some ideas for a few modifications in the store layout, but not significant changes. I poked my nose into all kinds of things over the last couple of days, and I haven't seen anything that hasn't impressed me. Frankly, Paul, I consider it an honor to be the buyer. You and Anna really created something marvelous."

"We modeled it after a huge store in Ohio…"

"*Ja*, where I did an apprenticeship," grinned Joseph. "I noticed the similarity right away. The tourism you attract is impressive, but I'd like to develop an online component to supplement the mail-order catalog sales."

The conversation centered on business, with both her aunt and uncle launching questions at Joseph with great excitement.

For a moment, Esther found herself thinking about her own future. She would now be working with Joseph on a regular basis. A week ago, she would have said he was one of two men from her past she never wanted to see again. Now that had changed. At least working with Joseph was better than seeing his brother Thomas, a man she loathed so much that the mere thought of him had her clenching her fork.

Her random thoughts focused when she heard Joseph say, "My sister will be so happy to learn I'll be here in Chaffinch from now on."

"How long has Miriam worked at the hospital?" she asked.

"Only a couple of months. Before that, she worked

at a hospital in Cleveland for two years, but she wanted to relocate to a smaller town. When an opening came up here, she took it."

"I'll have to go see her. We used to be such *gut* friends."

"I don't know if she knew you lived here, so it will be a nice surprise for her," replied Joseph.

"And what about your brother?" inquired Anna. "What was his name? Thomas?"

At Aunt Anna's innocent question, a heavy silence crashed into the room. Esther froze and grimaced. Anna gasped, then literally clapped a hand over her mouth, her eyes darting between Joseph and Esther.

"*Ach*, I'm sorry," she apologized.

Esther unscrunched her face, which had closed up in pain upon hearing Thomas's name. "It's okay, *aenti*," she said, trying to soothe Anna, who looked close to tears at the blunder. "He was bound to come up at some point or another."

"My brother is much the same as he always was," said Joseph in a hard voice. "He left the Amish, as you may know. Now that Miriam lives here, he may end up moving to Chaffinch as well. My sister tends to bail him out more than I think she should, but she has a soft heart. Thomas tends to follow her around like a puppy because he knows she'll help him get out of his difficulties. When she lived in Cleveland, well..." He trailed off and stared at his plate.

Esther realized her hand was still clenched on the fork. She made a deliberate effort to relax it lest anyone guess the extent to which the very name hurt her.

While Thomas was the one who had egged her toward her humiliation seven years before, she blamed

Joseph more for what happened afterward. He was the one who spread the incident around. He was the one who made sure everyone knew. He was the one, ultimately, who sent her fleeing away from Plum Grove.

Why, oh why, did it have to be Joseph who bought the store? Why couldn't it have been a stranger?

The false serenity she had attempted to cultivate over the last few days of working with Joseph became steeped with doubt. Could she keep up the facade of indifference? Could she pretend the past was gone and only the future mattered?

She had to. Her uncle counted on her. She needed to put the past behind her and look to the future. Lifting her head, Esther squared her shoulders and spoke into the silence. "Tell Uncle Paul and Aunt Anna what your plans are for making a website," she said.

It was all Joseph could do to refrain from cheering when Esther changed the subject. Covertly he watched the painful play of emotions on her face when Thomas's name was mentioned. He could almost follow her internal battle. And when she squared her shoulders, lifted her head and spoke about the store, he knew she had grown and matured to an amazing extent.

Thomas caused trouble wherever he went. He always had, even as a boy. For the life of him, Joseph didn't understand why his sister kept bailing Thomas out, but that was Miriam's business, not his. But he still blamed Thomas for the death of their parents, even though his brother was not directly responsible for their accident.

Worry impaired judgment, and his parents spent many years worrying over their youngest son's wildness and recklessness. When his father had steered their buggy directly into the path of an oncoming car, resulting in a hideous crash that ended his parents' lives, Joseph knew it had to be because his father was so distraught over his youngest son's latest exploits.

Joseph had not voluntarily spoken to his brother since the funeral six years ago.

Miriam kept him informed about their sibling, but even she knew he had no tolerance for hearing about Thomas.

So when Esther had changed the subject, he knew only too well the powerful amount of control it took. At that moment, he understood what a strong, mature woman Esther had become.

And he was glad he was getting to know her better.

Unaware of Joseph's line of thinking, Esther only knew she had to wait until he was gone before she could fall to pieces.

"Ach, *liebling*, I'm so sorry," her aunt said once again as they watched Joseph walk away from the house in the summer twilight. "I don't know what came over me to even mention that man's name."

Esther patted her aunt on the shoulder. "What's done is done, *aenti*. Don't worry about it."

"I'll wash up. Why don't you go work on your quilting?"

Esther kissed her aunt on the cheek. "*Ja, danke*. I think I will."

Her aunt knew good and well quilting is what Esther turned to when she was troubled. To offer to clean up meant her aunt knew Esther needed time alone.

She went upstairs to the bedroom that had become her sewing headquarters. A large quilting frame dominated one side of the room, a treadle sewing machine occupied the other. A broad table took up most of the center, a place she could lay out fabric pieces and move them around until she was satisfied with the patterns and design. Her uncle had built her a clever storage shelf, where she kept bolts of fabric, threads, pattern books and other accessories.

This was her world, her domain. The store dominated her waking hours, but this quilting room represented her passion.

She sighed and sat down before the quilting frame, where a colorful puzzle quilt lay nearly finished. All she needed was some extra hand-stitching along the center, and this quilt could be displayed in the store and hopefully sold.

So far she had sold every quilt she'd ever made. She sometimes jokingly complained to Aunt Anna that she didn't even have one of her own quilts to cover her bed because they were too valuable to keep.

But someday…someday she would make a quilt for herself. Her fingers applied the needle through fabric while her mind moved ahead to what that mythical quilt would look like. It would have her favorite colors, of course—earthy greens, creams, browns, a touch of red or blue or ochre here and there—and it would be a generous size to cover a large bed. A bed, she thought, that might someday hold her and her husband.

Without realizing it, her shoulders relaxed, and she felt peace flow back over her. Quilting always did that for her. It was her escape from troubles, her excuse to create, her time to pray. Quilting, to her, was a gift from *Gott*.

Despite her aunt and uncle's elation over Joseph's

offer to purchase the store, she knew they were concerned for her own peace of mind. It was up to Esther not to burden them with her insecurities and doubts.

And she wouldn't. She was blessed with skills—to manage the store, to create beautiful quilts—and she would use those skills to govern her emotions. She would not give in to childish regrets or painful memories of a situation that was over and done, and therefore could not be changed.

Armed with a better frame of mind, she reviewed her attitude toward Joseph as her needle moved in and out of the fabric stretched over the frame. Whatever difficulties he had caused her in the past, he was rescuing her aunt and uncle from a great burden in the present. She would conduct herself with decorum and dignity around him. For the sake of her aunt and uncle, whom she loved dearly, she would treat Joseph as if his past conduct had not occurred.

To his credit, he didn't seem any more inclined to dredge up painful memories than she was. If he continued to focus on the present and future—if he kept everything impersonal and professional—then she wouldn't have a problem working with him.

And she was forced to admit he was good at what he did. His research into the workings of the store was thorough and based on concrete facts and figures, customer flow and seasonal variations. She would just keep him at a professional distance and everything would be fine.

The one thing she didn't want to admit was how much he intrigued her on a personal level. To even admit such a thing seemed a betrayal of her youth. She remembered the way his eyes crinkled with amusement when the *Englisch* customer had tried to flirt with her and knew it meant he had a deep sense of humor, something she admired in a man.

Yes, she should keep things impersonal and objective between them. It was a tactic that had worked in the past. It would, *Gott* willing, work for the future as well.

Chapter Five

Esther settled into a decent working relationship with Joseph over the next week. She had meetings with his bankers, lawyers and accountants to process the paperwork necessary to sell the store.

"I wish this part was over, and I could get back to my normal routine," she grumbled after leaving one such meeting.

"I agree, it's an annoyance, but it's necessary." He cocked his head in her direction. "You didn't seem pleased with the accountant when he backed up my recommendation to upgrade to a computerized system."

"Of course not." She tried to keep annoyance out of her voice. "It's not the Plain way to use computers."

"No, but with the massive amount of inventory you juggle, it'll be far more efficient. I can't believe you managed all that for so many years by doing everything by hand." He helped her up into the buggy, then climbed into the seat behind her and flicked the horse's reins.

"I don't mind working with numbers," she said. "They're logical to me."

"Maybe that's why you like making quilts, especially your puzzle quilts. They're mathematical."

She managed a laugh. "I never thought about it, but you're right."

"Do you consider yourself mostly a logical person?"

"I do now." The moment the words left her lips, she could have kicked herself. She hadn't meant to reveal how harshly she had schooled herself to be cool, emotionless and rational after her angst-filled adolescence.

Sure enough, he picked up the slip of the tongue. "Now? You mean you weren't before?"

"It's something I grew into. I had to as I learned how to manage the store."

"Maybe so, but maybe that's why you're *gut* at it. You've cultivated a natural aptitude."

"*Ja*, true."

The horse clopped through town, where the extra-wide shoulders on the road had been designed to accommodate Amish traffic.

"I'm going to drop you at the store and then head for another appointment." Joseph guided the animal toward the front of the building. "I'll be back within a couple of hours."

"*Danke.*" She clutched her sheaf of paperwork and climbed down from the buggy and watched as he departed. She had spent a fair bit of time with Joseph over the last two weeks, and found him easy to work with. With the exception of knowing she would have to learn how to use a computer, the sale of the store was proceeding without much trouble because of his business acumen.

She smiled to herself and turned to enter the building. Sometimes it was hard to separate the boy she re-

membered from the man she now saw. The former she
detested; but the latter…well, there were times she even
came close to liking Joseph.

And after what happened in the past, that took some
mental gymnastics.

The store was busy but not terribly crowded. Esther dropped her paperwork in her office and headed
back out to the floor, where she could be most helpful.
She poked through corners, straightening displays and
neatening stock.

In one of the quieter corners of the store specializ-
ing in laundry items, she picked up a drying rack that
had been knocked over. The laundry area made decent
sales, but it didn't invite lingering, so not many people
were nearby when she heard a voice behind her.

"Hello."

She turned and saw a young *Englisch* man about her
age. He was dressed in regular clothes but was rather
scruffy around the edges. His body was soft and a bit
pudgy.

"Good afternoon," she replied. "May I help you with
something?"

"Don't you remember me, Esther?"

She peered closer. He had dark blue eyes and straight
brown hair, and did indeed look vaguely familiar. Without knowing why, her heart started beating in hard
thumps. "Should I?"

"I'm Thomas Kemp."

She blanched. To come face-to-face with him after
all these years…

She drew herself up and lifted her chin. "Hello,
Thomas."

He moved closer. "Come on. It's been a long time,

and all I get is a 'Hello, Thomas'? Surely you could do better than that."

"Of course I could do better." She kept her voice steely and controlled. "I could have you thrown out of the store. Would that work?"

"You wouldn't dare." He gave her a rakish grin she instantly hated. "Besides, on what grounds could you have me ejected? Just saying hello?"

"Is there something you want, Thomas? I can't imagine you're interested—" she gestured around her "—in learning how to do laundry by hand."

"Let's just say there's something in this department that's catching my interest right now." He moved closer.

Esther backed away. "There's nothing in here you want."

"Of course there is." He waggled his eyebrows.

"Thomas, leave me alone."

"Oh, come on. Is that any way to treat an old friend?"

"Friend?" She forced a laugh. "That's the last term I would apply to you."

"What do you say we go get a cup of coffee?" He moved closer.

She backed away. "I'm working."

"I just want to get to know you better."

"You know me just fine. Besides, do I have to quote the Bible to you?"

"Sure, quote away." He looked amused.

She snatched at the same verse she used before. "You have an unacceptable look on your face, so that means you've already committed adultery in your heart."

"Neither of us is married," he sneered, "so we're not committing adultery."

She was shocked he would so easily mock the Good

Book. Armed with her backup Bible verse, she said, "You're instructed to flee from youthful feelings and pursue righteousness and faith."

"Go back to the first part. That sounded more interesting." He moved forward.

She backed away. "Thomas, leave me alone. I have work to do."

"I'm just trying to…"

"You're trying my patience." Joseph spoke from behind.

Thomas whirled around. "Hello, Joseph."

"Little brother, it's time for you to go."

"Oh, have you already staked your claim on this one?" He jerked his head toward Esther.

She gasped at the presumption and shook her head in mute denial.

"Leave." Joseph crossed his arms and glared at his brother. "Because if you don't, I'm going to throw you out."

"You wouldn't dare." Thomas smirked.

Joseph moved with lightning speed. He grabbed his brother by the collar and began dragging him toward the back door of the store. Customers stopped and stared as the Amish man pulled on a shouting, resisting *Englisch* customer, but Joseph was stronger and in better physical shape than his brother. Thomas yelped and struggled, but he was no match for his brother's strength.

Joseph dragged him to the rear security door of the building. The door had a metal exit device that Joseph slammed open with his hip. He shoved his brother through the door and yanked it closed.

Dusting off his hands, he faced the curious onlookers. "Troublemaker," he explained to the crowd.

Esther didn't wait to see more. She sidled out through a different department and fled to her office. She locked the door behind her, then leaned against it, breathing heavily.

To be accosted on her own turf by the likes of Thomas was humiliating beyond anything she could imagine. While she was grateful for Joseph's rescue, it meant Thomas knew where she was—or at least, where she worked. She knew he could find out where she lived with very little effort. Would he accost her at home, too? In the garden? Was there any place safe?

Even as her mind raced through absurd and unrealistic scenarios, she knew she was being melodramatic. But the last—literally the last—person she ever expected to see again was Thomas.

"Esther?" Through the door, she heard Joseph's voice. He knocked. "Esther, are you in there?"

"Leave me alone."

"Are you *oll recht*? Did he hurt you?"

What do you care? was her unworthy thought. "I'm fine," she said out loud. "Just need to be alone for a while."

"Well, if you're sure…"

"*Ja*, I'm sure."

After a moment, she heard him walk away.

She felt like a wounded animal, crawling away into a hole to lick its injuries. She realized how much pain from her teenage years still remained. She'd thought herself healed, cured, healthy. Instead she found herself just as mortified as before, with emotions so raw and jagged that her breath came in gasps.

She needed to get away. She needed to talk with Aunt Anna.

Fishing a handkerchief from her pocket, she mopped her face and made sure her *kapp* wasn't askew. Then she lifted her chin, squared her shoulders, and went in search of Charles, her assistant manager.

"I'm going to go home," she told him. "Would you please cash out the registers and lock up for me after closing?"

"*Ja*, sure." He eyed her face. "Are you okay?"

"Just—just feeling a bit poorly, that's all." She gave him what she hoped was a reassuring smile, and turned to leave.

Once outside in the warm sunshine of early July, she looked around to make sure Thomas was nowhere in sight. Then she set off for home at a brisk walk.

When she arrived, she walked into the house through the kitchen door. Anna looked up, startled, a baking sheet of hot cookies in her gloved hands.

"Esther!" she cried. "Child, are you all right? What are you doing home so early?"

"Oh, Aunt Anna…" Her pent-up emotions burst through her defenses, and she dissolved into tears.

Anna dropped the cookie sheet on top the stove, yanked off her oven mitts, and pulled Esther into a hard embrace. "Shhh, shhh," she whispered, rocking as if Esther was a small child.

Esther clung to the older woman with desperation. She drew strength from her aunt's solid figure.

When Esther's tears subsided, Anna led Esther toward a kitchen chair and pushed her down. Esther sat, then dropped her head in her hands as her aunt sat opposite her.

"Now tell me what happened, *liebling*," Anna ordered.

Esther sniffed and mopped her face with her handkerchief. "Thomas came into the store."

Anna's eyes widened. "Thomas Kemp? Joseph's brother?"

"*Ja.* He more or less accosted me in the laundry section, backed me into a corner and said he wanted to get to know me better."

"Then what happened?"

"Joseph came up from behind him and literally threw him out of the store."

"Did he?" Anna's eyes danced, and a smile hovered on her lips. "I don't condone violence, but I'm glad he did that."

Esther responded with a faint smile of her own. "*Ja*, me too. Joseph made something of a scene in front of some customers because Thomas didn't go quietly, and he shoved him out the back door of the store, which, as you know, automatically locks from the inside."

"And he didn't try to come back in the front?"

"Not that I know of, but I really didn't stay around to find out. I closed myself into the office, and when Joseph knocked on the office door to see if I was okay, I just told him to go away." She sniffed. "I couldn't stay at the store and pretend nothing had happened, so I came home."

"And Joseph—did he raise any painful memories? Did he make any mention of what happened when you were seventeen?"

"He exists. Therefore he raises painful memories," quipped Esther in a sour voice. "But, no, he didn't make any other reference to the last time Thomas and I had an encounter. Nor what he did to make it ten times worse."

Anna shook her head and murmured, "Honestly, Esther, it just doesn't seem fitting with his character."

"Whose, Joseph's?"

"*Ja.* It's hard to see the professional business man today as the same man who did you so wrong when you were younger."

"Well, he *is* the same man." Esther's voice was hard and unforgiving. "He alludes to it once in a while, but neither of us has tackled it head-on. I promised I wouldn't do anything to jeopardize the sale of the store, and I haven't. But sometimes it's hard to bite my tongue."

"And Thomas…" Anna paused. "Joseph did mention he might try to follow Miriam here to Chaffinch since Miriam tends to bail him out of his troubles again and again." She shook her head. "I remember their parents, they were fine people. How they managed to hatch as bad a character as Thomas, I'll never know."

"And why everybody had to end up following me here to Chaffinch is another mystery," Esther retorted. "I thought I was safe here with you and Uncle Paul. I built up a whole new life here, and now it's crashing down around me again."

"No, it's not." Anna's voice was firm. "You're a well-respected and baptized member of the church. No one knows what happened when you were seventeen, and no one will. Miriam won't say anything, I'm sure. Neither will Joseph. As for Thomas—well, since he's unlikely to ever darken the door of our Sunday services, his voice won't be heard."

"*Ja,* I suppose you're right." Esther wrung the handkerchief in her hands. "But don't you think it's unfair and coincidental that the whole family should end up here, of all places? Maybe *Gott* is playing a joke on me."

"Or, maybe *Gott* has plans for forgiveness. Joseph seems to have grown out of any adolescent peccadillos. From what he says, Miriam sounds like she turned out well, even if she did jump the fence. As for Thomas— well, the Lord has redeemed worse people than Thomas. There's always hope."

"And you're always the optimist," remarked Esther. She gave her aunt a shaky smile. "It's one of the many reasons I love you."

"Here comes your uncle in from the garden." Anna rose. "Why don't you go upstairs and do some quilting? That always calms you down. I'll give your uncle an explanation of why you're home."

"*Ja*, I will. *Danke*." She leaned over, kissed her aunt on the cheek and retreated up the stairs.

Once inside her sanctuary—as she sometimes jokingly termed the quilting room—she sank down on the chair before the sewing machine. Thomas, redeemed? The thought was laughable. She'd grown up with the Kemp family, and Thomas had been heading down the wrong path for as long as she could remember.

Why, at age seventeen, she had let him sweet-talk her into taking off her dress in a moment of adolescent curiosity, she never knew. She never had any romantic interest in Thomas, but hormones did strange things to teenagers. She knew things could have escalated into something more, had not Joseph discovered them and saved her from total ruination.

But then, having done that, he proceeded to spread rumors about her indiscretion far and wide, rumors which made it impossible to hold her head up.

At last, when the church gossip became more than she could bear, she had written to her aunt and uncle begging for refuge. Uncle Paul's health was starting to get wobbly about then, and they both welcomed the opportunity to not just have her stay with them but to work in the store. Esther's gratitude had never diminished.

Esther sighed and rose to examine a new quilt she was assembling on the table. This was one of her jigsaw puzzle quilts, and she had set herself a challenge to make the puzzle pieces small and then arrange the colors of the pieces into a secondary design within the quilt—a pattern within a pattern. It was just the kind of mathematical challenge she enjoyed.

She moved and arranged and played with pieces, lost in the intricacy of it, and forgot about the complications of her personal life for a while. An hour later, when her aunt called her down to dinner, she snapped to the present and realized the quilt pieces were in a beautiful arrangement—concentric diamond patterns with subtle gradations of color, coming to a pinpoint of black in the exact center.

She'd never seen such an arrangement on any quilt, and she lingered for a moment, looking it over, trying to decide if she wanted to alter anything more or keep it exactly as it was.

If only, she thought, she could arrange her life as meticulously and precisely as she could arrange a quilt.

Uncle Paul eyed her as she entered the kitchen. "Feeling better?" he inquired.

"Much better." She pecked him on the cheek. "Quilting always relaxes me. You should see the pattern I just finished working on—I think it's very unique."

"Are you going to sell it when it's done?" asked Anna, putting platters of food on the table.

"*Ja*, probably." She paused for a silent blessing, then reached for a bowl of corn. "I do think it's ironic that I never keep any of my own quilts."

"You will, someday. But quilts are some of the best-selling items in the store."

"For certain and sure. I sold another one today. They aren't cheap either."

"Now let's discuss something more serious." Uncle Paul rested his fork on his plate. "Tell me, do we need to beef up security in the store? Do you feel threatened because Thomas is back in town?"

Her appetite disappearing, Esther sighed. "I don't know. Joseph was quite rough with him when he threw him out the back door. I don't know what kind of man Thomas is now—if he was just there to make a scene because he enjoys it or if he is bent on retaliation. I guess it's something I'll have to discuss with Joseph tomorrow—even though it's *not* an issue I wanted to bring up," she added bitterly.

"Joseph is going to have to deal with it," said Anna. "It's his responsibility, for several reasons. One, he's buying the store. Two, it's his brother. And three, if he wants you to continue to be the manager, he's going to have to make sure you're not feeling so threatened or unsafe that you can't do your job."

"*Ja*. You're right." Esther pushed her food around on her plate. "I guess I was hoping we could manage this whole transition without ever dredging up the past, but obviously that's not realistic."

"Don't forget, *liebling*," said Paul gently. "You're not a teenager anymore, and neither is Joseph. You're both adults, and professionals. If Joseph is forced to handle the issue of his brother, I'm confident he'll do it in a way that is not humiliating to you."

"In other words," added Anna, "the burden is on him, not you. What's past is past. You can't undo what happened seven years ago, and neither can Joseph. Neither can Thomas, for that matter. Now the only thing that counts is how you conduct yourself in the future."

"Which," said Esther with resignation, "means I shouldn't be running away from the store whenever Thomas shows his face."

"I don't think anyone blames you for needing to get away," asserted her uncle. "Especially if Thomas got too close for comfort. Not to mention he caught you totally by surprise. But as the saying goes, forewarned is forearmed. Think ahead what you might do if he comes back in, and plan accordingly."

Esther knew this was the way her uncle's mind worked. He called it "scenario building," a technique by which he thought through many different contingency plans depending on the situation. Over the years, she'd seen him handle any number of issues in the store with calmness and efficiency, simply because he had "scripted" the problem ahead of time and already thought through a plan of action. It was a skill she admired.

"*Ja*, you're right," she agreed. "I'll think about what to do if Thomas returns to bother me. I'll also think of how to handle it if—no, make that *when*—Joseph brings up the subject of why I left Plum Grove seven years ago. It's bound to come up anyway."

"That's my girl," said Uncle Paul with approval. He

patted her hand. "No wonder you make such an excellent manager."

She smiled at his praise. "*Danke*, both of you. You always have been my rock in times of trouble."

She was able to tackle her dinner with a better appetite – after thanking *Gott* for the emotional support He had given her in the form of her aunt and uncle.

Chapter Six

Armed with the scenarios she worked through in her mind overnight, Esther walked to work the next day toting an umbrella for what looked to be incoming rain. She entered the store, prepared to handle whatever came her way.

Sure enough, Joseph cornered her immediately. "Are you all right? I was worried after you went home so early yesterday."

"Fine. Thomas didn't hurt me—he just shook me up." She kept calm and refused to let the memory unsettle her.

"Well, if you're sure…"

"I'm sure. Don't fuss, Joseph. But I do appreciate the show of strength in booting your brother out the back door." A glimmer of humor touched her lips.

He looked at her for a long moment. Esther tried not to interpret his expression as admiring. She didn't want to respond to Joseph, not in any personal way.

A rumble of thunder could be heard in the distance.

"Rain's coming," commented Esther, anxious to divert the conversation away from yesterday's incident.

"That will put a damper on the tourists. It should be quieter today."

"Don't the buses drive in the rain?" He raised his eyebrows, and Esther had a feeling he knew she was changing the subject. "I would think the tourists would come in regardless of the weather."

"Some do, of course, but a surprising number stay home when it's wet. The reason is most people like to look around the whole town and visit all the stores, not just this one. Rain tends to slow that down."

"I see. And if things are slower in the store, what do you normally do?"

"Restocking. That's mostly what I do on rainy days." She smoothed down her apron. "What will you be doing?"

"Restocking, of course." He quirked a grin at her.

She caught her breath. His rare smiles tended to knock the wind out of her. She made sure her voice was steady. "No meetings with accountants or lawyers?"

"Not today. So why don't you show me what needs doing, and I'll get busy."

"*Ja*, sure. I'll ask Charles to bring in what he has from the warehouse."

The assistant manager trundled over the new merchandise to be restocked, and for the next several hours, Esther, Joseph and various store employees refilled the shelves.

In the early afternoon, a couple entered the store dressed in *Englischer* clothing. The man wore a baseball cap; the woman carried a large purse.

The man swaggered in, stopped and planted his hands on his hips. "What a stupid place!" he announced, looking around.

"Yes, I agree!" his female companion proclaimed loudly.

Esther raised her eyebrows as she watched the couple. What an odd thing to do. What were they both up to?

"Wow, look at this overpriced schlock," said the man in a loud voice, which carried. He poked at a display of gardening tools. Several customers turned to look at him, and all the store employees stopped what they were doing to watch him as well.

"I haven't seen this much garbage since we went into that pawn shop yesterday," declared the woman. She, too, prodded a display, this one of handmade soaps.

"This floor squeaks," continued the man, trodding back and forth on an ancient board, worn with age, beneath his feet.

"And what about this?" The woman gestured toward the display of quilts. "Have you even seen anything so pathetic?"

"And overpriced!" sneered the man, batting at a tag attached to some cast iron cookware. "Everything costs too much."

Esther didn't know whether to be alarmed or amused by the strange behavior. "May I help you?" she asked, walking closer to the couple.

"No. Just looking," the man retorted. "Go away."

Partly entertained, partly baffled, Esther watched the couple as they complained their way across the store. Nothing met with their approval. The aisles were too wide or too narrow. The merchandise was too expensive or too cheap. The departments were too spacious or too cramped. She trailed behind, observing their loud and attention-grabbing complaints. Why were they even in the store if all they were going to do was criticize?

The couple soon moved apart into different areas. Esther signaled to Joseph, who had been stocking shelves in a different part of the store and was unaware of this new development.

"Troublemakers," she whispered to him. "Watch them. If you go over there and keep an eye on the man, I'll stay here and keep an eye on the woman."

He nodded and moved off to discretely trail the man.

After a while, Esther noticed it was the man doing most of the complaining and being the most obnoxious. He also drew all the attention, as both customers and store clerks watched him.

His female companion, in contrast, fell silent. She moved around the shelves seemingly at random. Then, quick as a wink, she slipped a small container of hand-made skin balm into her sleeve. After a moment, she shook her sleeve and the balm fell into the open mouth of her purse.

Watching her from the end of the aisle, Esther crossed her arms and said nothing.

The woman glanced around, glared at Esther and moved into another aisle. Esther watched her through cracks between the shelving units. Soon a packet of hand-embroidered linen napkins joined the container of balm inside the woman's purse. Then a lace doily. Then a small scented candle. The woman continued harvesting items from the shelves, seemingly unaware she was being watched.

Esther moved around, caught Joseph's eye and jerked her head toward the woman. He nodded in instant comprehension.

The couple started to make their way toward the front of the store once more. Joseph slipped around various displays and placed himself near the cash register. Esther went and stood right in front of the doorway.

"Yeah, nothing in here of any interest," the man trumpeted. He stopped in front of Joseph, near the cash register. "Are you the manager? If so, let me tell you, this is the biggest collection of garbage I've seen in years."

"Then why are you here?" inquired Joseph.

"Because I've heard how great this store is, but I'm here to tell you differently."

"I'm sorry you didn't find things to your satisfaction." Joseph smiled and kept his tone pleasant.

"What are you going to do about it?" demanded the man. "Aren't you going to try to salvage my experience?"

"Salvage your experience?" Joseph raised his eyebrows. "And how should I do that?"

"I dunno, maybe you should give me a discount or something."

"A discount on what? You just told me we have the biggest collection of garbage you've seen in years." His tone remained calm.

"You Amish," sneered the man. "Too wimpy even to defend your own businesses."

"Don't forget cowardly and spineless," Joseph added.

Esther marveled that Joseph had the guts to mock the man.

The belligerent stranger grew even more pugnacious and threatening. "Are you insulting me?" he demanded.

"Not at all. I'm just wondering why you're in this store."

"Just here to laugh at you weirdos." The man swaggered right up to Joseph, and for one horrified moment Esther thought the stranger was going to haul off and slug him.

Meanwhile, the woman sidled closer to the exit. Esther saw her and moved to block the doorway.

"Get out of my way," she snarled.

"Certainly," replied Esther. Emulating Joseph, she kept her voice calm. "As soon as you unload all the stolen items from your purse."

"Stolen items? How dare you accuse me of stealing anything?"

"Ma'am, I watched you. Your purse is full of stolen goods. I would appreciate it if you would return them."

"You can't prove anything."

"On the contrary, our security cameras have captured everything," Esther lied smoothly.

"Security cameras?" scoffed the woman. "What Amish store uses security cameras?"

"This Amish store does. Now, ma'am, please empty your purse before we call the police."

"Using a telephone? I thought the Amish didn't have them."

The man peeled away from Joseph and stormed over to Esther. "What's going on here?"

"This lady is accusing me of stealing," whined the woman.

"Are you threatening my wife?" roared the man.

Esther drew herself up. "Not at all. I simply requested she empty her purse of all the items she stole."

"That's threatening," he snarled. "We're leaving."

Before Esther could respond, before Joseph could reach her, the man gave Esther a powerful two-handed shove which slammed her into a display unit near the exit. He and the woman pushed open the store's front door and ran off.

Caught off balance, Esther stumbled and fell against the display unit and crashed to the floor.

Several of the other customers and store clerks screamed. Esther rolled over and noticed her *kapp* had fallen off.

Joseph was at her side in an instant. He pulled her to her feet. "You're hurt."

"I am?" She felt dull and clumsy. She wiped her eyes and felt sticky blood on her fingers.

Employees clustered around her, murmuring comforting words, while shocked customers observed the drama from a distance and whispered together.

Joseph whipped a handkerchief from his pocket and carefully wiped her forehead. "Head wounds bleed like crazy, but I think that's the only injury."

"I'm okay." Esther's legs trembled in delayed shock, but she kept her voice calm. "Don't fuss so, Joseph."

"You should see yourself," he replied with a grim smile. "You look like you were beat up in a dark alley. Come in back. You need to sit down."

He slipped a strong arm around her waist, and Esther didn't argue. She didn't want to admit how good that arm felt.

Joseph leaned down to snatch up Esther's *kapp*, then supported her down the length of the store to the back office.

"Sit down," he said, pushing her gently into an office chair. "I'm going to go get a wet cloth and the first aid kit. You need to get cleaned up."

He closed the office door behind him to give Esther some privacy. Left alone for a moment, he closed his eyes and pinched the bridge of his nose. How could he have left her to deal with the shoplifters? The sight of her covered with blood shook him more than he wanted to admit.

He straightened up and went in search of the first aid kit.

When he reentered the office, he brought with him a few damp washcloths and the small emergency kit kept behind the register. "Nice to have a whole inventory to choose from," he quipped, indicating the small towels. "These came from the kitchen department. How do you feel?"

"A bit shaky," she admitted. "Like somebody's been pushing me around." Wry humor laced her words.

"Well, if you can joke about it, I guess I don't need to take you in to the doctor."

"No, not at all. But you did the smart thing to get me off the floor. The last thing customers need to see is a bloody and battered manager."

He wrung out one of the washcloths, squatted down and began dabbing her forehead. "Let me know if it hurts."

She said nothing until Joseph got to the cut on her forehead. Then she winced. "Ouch, that stings."

"Okay, that's the source. Sorry to hurt you, but I couldn't see how bad it was with all the blood around." He rinsed and rewrung the washcloth, then swabbed around the cut with an alcohol wipe from the first aid kit. "I don't think it needs stitches," he stated, "but it's still bleeding. Here, press this to the cut while I clean off the rest of your face." He gave her a gauze pad.

Esther kept her eyes directed downward, but even so he sensed the intimacy of his actions. He noticed the pulse in her throat and wondered if it was solely due to her encounter with the thieves.

She sighed. "I hope you're not getting the wrong impression about how often things like this happen."

"*Nee*, but it *has* been a rough couple of days. Especially for you."

"I'm angry those people were such blatant shoplifters."

"Not as angry as I am at myself," replied Joseph. "I should have been the one standing at the door. I'm kicking myself that you're the one they knocked down, not me."

"I didn't expect it myself, so how could you? I thought I'd be blocking just the woman, not both of them."

"I wonder how long they rehearsed that routine before coming in here." Joseph shook his head. "What did she steal, did you see?"

Esther gave a small snort of laughter. "Minor stuff, really. Hand balm. Soap. A doily. A couple of candles. Things like that."

"Seems like a lot of trouble for maybe twenty-five dollars' worth of merchandise. Not to mention the whole show they put on to distract attention."

"Some people have strange hobbies."

"How often does this kind of thing happen?"

"Shoplifting? Sometimes. It's the cost of doing business. Violent shoplifting? Rarely."

"You bluffed about the security cameras to the woman, but maybe we should install some."

"First computers, now security cameras." She met his eyes. "Is that the Amish way?"

"No, but you could chalk it up to the cost of doing business." He gave her a small smile.

"We already have a silent alarm that summons the police."

"You do?" His eyebrows rose. "Have you ever had to use it?"

"Just once, not long after I arrived here in Chaffinch. A man started beating his child over in the toy department. Two of our employees held him while Aunt Anna used the silent alarm. The good thing about being in a small town is the police were here within minutes."

Joseph gave a low whistle. "Wow."

"*Ja*, it was a crazy day. But for the most part, things are peaceful. We're not the usual target for shoplifting because we don't carry valuable merchandise."

"Sure, it's valuable…"

"Not to thieves. Most crooks want to steal something they want for themselves or something they can sell for money on a street corner. Who is going to want to buy a lace doily or a bar of handmade soap?"

"I see your point." He nodded and kept cleaning off the blood across her cheeks and chin. "I suppose the only merchandise that would fall under that category is the knives—pocket knives, utility knives, that kind of thing. And I notice you keep those under glass."

"*Ja*, but that's mostly for public safety. We can't risk children grabbing one and hurting themselves."

"Here, let's see if that cut is still bleeding." Joseph peeled back the piece of gauze Esther had been holding to her forehead. He examined the wound for a moment. "*Ja*, it's still bleeding. Once it slows down, I'll put a real bandage on it, but go ahead and keep applying pressure."

"I'm going to have to go home and change my dress," Esther said, looking down at her bloodstained garment.

"Your poor aunt and uncle. You're going to give them quite a shock showing up like this."

"But at least my face will be cleaned up." She raised one arm, still sticky with blood. "But I'll have to wash my hands."

"How are you feeling?"

"Better. I think the shock has passed."

He peeked under the gauze pressed to her forehead again. "It's slowing down. I think we can try applying a bandage now." He rummaged through the small plastic box. "Do you have any other first aid kits? I don't see what we need in this one."

"We have several. There's one in the staff bathroom. I'll go get it, and I'll wash off my hands and arms at the same time."

"*Ja*, sure." He rose from his squatting position.

Esther stood up and gasped. She swayed and looked ready to fall.

Joseph grabbed her by the arms. "Whoa. Sit down."

She sat. "I didn't expect that."

"To be dizzy? I'm not surprised. You had quite a shock. And the cut is bleeding again." He pulled out a clean bit of gauze from the kit and applied it once again to her forehead.

Ministering to Esther affected Joseph more than he expected. It didn't feel like an impersonal manager assisting an injured employee. It felt far more intimate. Esther kept her eyes downcast, and he saw a pulse beating in her throat.

How could this woman be the same girl whose reputation was in ruins seven years ago? When she disappeared from Plum Grove so soon after he found her with his brother, it wasn't hard to draw an unpleasant conclusion.

Yet it seemed he was wrong. Since coming here to Chaffinch, he had caught no hint of scandal, no whiff of disgrace, nothing that might indicate Esther's hasty departure had been due to anything more than embarrassment.

He found himself relieved because he was becoming far more interested in Esther than was professionally appropriate.

"If you can hold this to your forehead, I'll go look for that first aid kit," Joseph said as he rose.

Esther applied pressure to the gauze pad. "If you look below the bathroom sink, it's a large white box strapped on the side of the cabinet."

"I'll find it." He slipped out of the office.

His reaction to her nearness didn't bode well. He couldn't possibly be interested in Esther. She had made it clear she hated him for his role in her adolescent misadventure. Yet he found he liked the idea of earning her trust—and forgiveness.

He rummaged under the bathroom sink and located the larger first aid kit with ease, then returned to the office. "How are you feeling?" he inquired. "Still dizzy?"

"I haven't tried to stand up again, so I don't know." She removed the gauze. "I think the bleeding is slowing down again, though."

"Let me see what size bandage would best fit." He opened the kit and looked through the options. He pulled out a larger gauze pad, some surgical tape, and a tube of antibiotic ointment as well. "This should work."

He dried her forehead with a clean dry washcloth, then squeezed a generous dollop of ointment on the pad. "The bleeding has nearly stopped. Ready?" he said as he applied the large bandage to her forehead.

Esther touched the dressing. "Feels awkward, but it's better than bleeding all over myself, I suppose."

"Ja." He rose, then held out his arms. "Let's get you into the bathroom to wash up, then I'm going to take you home. You can't appear in front of customers in a bloodstained dress."

Esther took his hands and rose to her feet. Joseph kept his grip on her while she tested herself for steadiness. His hands were warm and firm.

"Okay?" he inquired.

"Ja, seems to be." She released his hands and took a few steps. "No dizziness."

"If you want to wash up, I'll go talk to the assistant manager. I'm sure he's wondering if you're okay anyway."

"Go, I'll be fine."

"Don't, ah, be too shocked by your appearance." His voice held some dry mirth. "You're a sight."

He departed for the main room of the store while Esther headed toward the washroom.

Joseph located Charles, the assistant manager. "I'm going to take Esther home," he informed the younger man.

"How is she?" Charles looked worried.

"A little shaken, but she'll be okay. But for obvious reasons, she shouldn't be seen by customers. Plus she's had a shock."

"Do you want to use my buggy? It won't take long to hitch up."

"Danke!" Joseph smiled. No wonder Esther had so much faith in her assistant manager. "That will be a big help. I don't know if she can walk all the way home."

"I'll go hitch up."

Joseph turned back toward the office. Esther was just emerging from the washroom. "Ready?" he asked.

She turned. *"Ja.* And before you ask, I feel okay. Steady. I won't faint."

"I'll still drive you back, though. Charles offered me his buggy. He's hitching up the horse right now."

"Ja, danke."

Joseph walked with Esther out the building's side door into the parking area, where Charles stood holding the horse's head. Rain pattered down, dampening the pavement and sending up a warm, humid smell.

"You okay, Esther?" Charles inquired. He eyed her large bandage and bloodstained dress.

"Ja," she replied. "But as you can see, I can't go back to work. At least not until I've changed my clothes."

"Not until tomorrow at least," Joseph said. He assisted Esther into the buggy. *"Vielen dank* for the loan of your buggy, Charles."

"Not a problem." Charles touched his hat brim. "Just stay home and rest," he told Esther.

"Danke. I will." She smiled at him.

Joseph climbed into the buggy, took the reins, and clucked to the horse.

"Danke for taking care of me, Joseph." Esther sighed and leaned back in the buggy.

He gave her a sidelong glance. "I'll always be here to take care of you."

And he meant it. He found himself always wanting to take care of her.

Chapter Seven

I'll always be here to take care of you.

Those words echoed in Esther's head during the week following her encounter with the violent shoplifters. She had analyzed the statement every possible way from every possible angle, but she wasn't any closer to understanding its meaning.

Or perhaps she shied away from the one meaning she didn't want to hear. Perhaps Joseph was coming to mean a lot to her on a personal level, and she balked at that conclusion. It just didn't seem right for her to become interested in the person who had helped ruin her reputation as a teen.

The beautiful puzzle quilt was finished. She looked it over, sighed, then folded it up and slipped it into the oversize cloth bag she kept for protecting her quilts while ferrying them to the store.

"Are you sure you want to sell this one?" Aunt Anna poked at the bag.

"To be honest, I have mixed feelings about it," Esther said. "I put a lot of work into making this one."

What she couldn't admit was the real reason behind

her ambivalence about parting with the quilt. Not only was it the most unique and unusual project she had ever made, but she'd spent so much time thinking about Joseph during its construction that it seemed his entire presence was imbued within the colorful squares and beautiful pattern.

On second thought, maybe it was best if she sold it. Joseph had become such an integral part of her professional life, and now with her aunt and uncle's constant praise for him, he was infiltrating her personal life as well. She wasn't sure she wanted that.

"Ask Joseph if he can come for dinner tonight," said Uncle Paul.

She smiled. Her aunt and uncle's admiration for Joseph had increased dramatically since her injury. When Joseph had brought her home, they had clucked and fussed over her, and thanked Joseph for his aid when she'd needed it. Now, in their eyes, he could do no wrong.

"Have him for dinner so you can thank him again?" she said, teasing them.

Her uncle grinned. "*Ja*, sure. But we also want to talk business. Plus, your aunt has a new recipe she wants to try out."

"*Oll recht*, I'll ask him," Esther said.

Setting out for the store, she pulled a wagon behind her holding the bagged quilt. When she arrived in town, she pulled the wagon up the ramp to the store's wide porch area and unlocked the doors. She unwrapped the quilt and laid it on the cash register counter while she pulled the wagon out of sight into a back room.

Gradually employees began filtering in and setting up for the day's sales. When Joseph walked in shortly before opening, Esther had to admit she was waiting for him. Anticipating his arrival. Looking forward to seeing him.

"Aunt Anna wants to invite you to dinner tonight," she told him. "She says she has a new recipe she wants to try out."

"That's nice of her." Joseph touched the quilt still folded on the cash register counter. "What's this?"

"Oh, my latest quilt. I thought about keeping it, but I think I'll sell it instead."

"May I look?"

"Ja."

He partially unfolded the quilt. "This is beautiful, Esther. I'm surprised you could part with it."

"I can always make another. I thought about putting it here." She walked over to the quilting section and touched the display stands, where folded quilts were exhibited on stout rods.

"No." He shook his head. "It's going up there." He pointed to the wall, where quilts could be displayed full scale.

Esther experienced a quiver of concern. "That seems too prideful."

"You didn't make the decision, I did. Trust me, this quilt won't be around for long. Maybe a day or two at most. Then someone will buy it."

"Well, if you're sure…"

She helped him remove the existing quilt on display and replace it with her own quilt. When she finally stepped back and was able to see the full thing, she was pleased.

She turned to see Joseph studying her. "It's an amazing piece of work," he said.

She blushed. "I don't want to seem *hochmut*."

"Then I won't praise it any more. But how did you come up with the design?"

"I just played with it until it seemed right."

"I think that's your mathematical aptitude showing. You'll have to make more quilts like this."

She studied her handiwork. "If I do make more, I might alter it a bit, perhaps with more earthy colors. Greens, browns, beige, rust, a touch of red…"

"You said before those were your favorite color combinations."

"*Ja.* I don't know why, but I find them peaceful and soothing."

"Does this quilt have a message?"

She turned and looked at him. "What do you mean?"

"It's something I heard, that many quilters have a sort of message or theme that gets built into the pattern or colors. Almost like a hidden language."

She turned away. How unusual that he would know of that. "They're called message quilts," she said. "It's when an emotion or a statement is incorporated into the artwork of the quilt. Sometimes a quilt tells a story or relates some family history. That kind of thing."

"Do you incorporate messages with your quilts?"

"Sometimes."

"What kinds of messages?"

"I've made wedding quilts," she replied. "The message is for love and fidelity. I've made baby quilts. I've made baptismal quilts."

"But you've never made a quilt for yourself."

"No. I… I haven't had time." For her, quilting was a deeply personal art form, and she didn't feel like expressing to this man how she worked through her emotions by piecing together fabric. Nor did she care to share her changing feelings for him.

"But if you ever did make a quilt for yourself, would it be a puzzle quilt?"

"Probably. It's the pattern I'm most comfortable using, and I enjoy playing with different designs within it, but I don't know if I could ever claim it would have a message."

A bell jangled over the front door of the store. The first customer of the day had arrived.

The morning was busy as tourists came in. To her amusement, Esther noted clusters of women stopping in front of the quilt display to gape at her creation. She overheard comments and praise. Most of them seemed to be from people who appreciated the art behind the design. Even a few men stopped to admire the mathematical precision of the pattern.

Two middle-aged women spent a long time lingering in front of it. Finally, one of the women said to the other, "That's it. I've got to have it."

"I've never seen anything like it," her companion said. "Imagine, using jigsaw puzzle shapes that interlock, and then create a pattern within a pattern."

The first woman came over to where Esther was manning the cash register. "Excuse me, miss, I'd like to buy that quilt."

She smiled. If the quilt had to sell, at least it was selling to someone who understood the creative process behind the work. "*Ja*, let me get someone to help get it down."

She fetched Joseph from another part of the store. "You're right," she whispered. "It didn't last long."

With his help, she removed the quilt from the wall and folded it, then brought it to the cash register.

The buyer peered closer at the quilt, examining it with an air of authority. "Worth every penny," she finally proclaimed. "Whoever made this is a genuine artist."

Joseph winked at Esther. She bit back a smile.

"I'm a little jealous," admitted the buyer's friend. "I wish I'd seen it first, or I would have bought it."

"We have special order forms," suggested Esther. She reached beneath the counter and took out some pre-printed forms. "If you want a similar quilt, I'm sure the quilter would be happy to make one for you."

"Are you certain they're Amish quilts?" inquired the second woman with a hint of suspicion. "I only want an Amish quilt."

"Yes, ma'am," replied Esther. "I can guarantee that it will be made by an Amish woman."

"Then, yes, I'd like one too."

Esther spent a few minutes filling in the required information—size, pattern, colors—and the woman paid half the money down. Then both women, chattering in excitement, gathered up the quilt and left the store.

"I didn't know you made custom quilts," observed Joseph.

"*Ja*, sure, I've been making them for years. Lots of the quilters do, not just myself. That's why I had these forms printed."

"Why aren't those forms out where everyone can see them?"

"Well, uh…"

Joseph looked at the quilting section, tapping his chin thoughtfully. "Changes," he finally pronounced.

"We've talked about expanding the quilting section, but now I'm going to get started on it. They need to be featured more."

Esther had to fight back the irrational feeling that she was being criticized. She knew Joseph's job was to implement changes that would maximize profits for the store. His suggestions were not meant to disparage her management style.

"I'm the one that put the quilt section in a few years ago," she informed him. "Before that, Uncle Paul just had them folded on a shelf among the other linens we sell."

"Then you were right to create a display area. But trust me, making it even bigger will be a success."

"If you think so…"

"I've looked at the numbers. I've seen how many quilts you sell in a week. We can ramp that up by displaying more." He pointed to the setup. "For example, we'll make larger partitions to create three walls for displaying an entire quilt, not just one. And I'm thinking about a quilting station, where quilts under production can be made so people can learn about the process."

She voiced her doubts. "Do you really think there's that much interest?"

Joseph countered with logic. "I've spent enough time among the *Englisch* to understand they appreciate handmade goods. That's why they're coming into the store. That's why that woman was so insistent the quilt be made by Amish hands. I don't think you appreciate how widespread that sentiment is."

"But why are you so focused on quilts? We have so many different kinds of products in the store."

"Because quilts are eye-catching. They're what tourists expect to see too. Might as well give them what they want."

Esther wasn't sure she liked the direction this conversation was taking, but neither could she think of any way to disagree with his reasoning.

He seemed to pluck her thoughts out of the air. "You don't approve?"

"I didn't say that." Esther picked up a cloth and started dusting the glass-topped counter. "But it does seem contrary to our beliefs to be so interested in money."

"*Ja*, maybe. But my goal is not to become wealthy, my goal is to make the store profitable to benefit everyone. As a manager, you must know how many people depend on the store for their income. Don't you think it best to make the store as profitable as possible so they can make a living?"

"*Ja*. When you put it that way, I suppose you're right."

Smiling, Joseph said, "I'd like to bring up the subject this evening with your aunt and uncle."

"My uncle, especially." Esther chuckled as she looked up. "He loves to discuss store improvements."

Sure enough, that evening after the silent blessing on the meal, Joseph raised the issue with Uncle Paul and Aunt Anna.

"Expand the quilting area, eh?" Paul chewed thoughtfully on a piece of meat. "*Ja*, I can see how that would be an advantage."

"I'm interested in more than just expanding it," Joseph clarified. "Considering how much interest there is in handmade quilts, I'd like to set up the area as a quilting station. It could include not just finished quilts on display but some of the stages a quilt goes through while it's being made. In fact, if I could talk someone into it, I'd hold demonstrations." He looked at Esther. "Would you consider working on a quilt while in the store? Or would someone you know consider it?"

She shook her head. "My concern is that it will invite photography, not to mention praise. Too much *hochmut*, whether it's me or someone else."

"*Ja*, I can see that." Joseph rubbed his chin, considering.

"But you can compromise," inserted Aunt Anna. "Have a quilt in progress. Show it on a quilting frame. You can have the phases of production laid out in a demonstration. Like museums do."

"That would be better," agreed Joseph. "We could make a work in progress–type display, along with signage and a colored mock-up illustration of what the quilt will look like when it's finished as a way to encourage interest. And if forms are placed in a prominent location, then we can take orders."

"Maybe make some dummy quilt squares," added Uncle Paul, "and invite people to arrange them on a tabletop as a sort of hands-on example of how patterns are arranged."

"*Ja!*" said Esther. "There could be two areas for that kind of interaction, one for adults and even a scaled-down version in the children's area."

"Children's area—*ja*, quilt blocks and a tabletop area for arranging them is an excellent idea," said Joseph. "I'll bet we could even get one of our vendors to put together a small beginner's quilting kit for children, with the blocks already made, and all the necessary components in the kit. A quilt in a box, so to speak."

"Evelyn Miller, I'll bet she would do something like that," offered Anna. "She often makes children's toys, and she quilts too."

And so the meal continued, with Esther and her aunt and uncle brainstorming ideas with Joseph.

She admired Joseph's business acumen. Suddenly, she understood why he was so insistent on expanding this one department. Having managed the store for several years now and witnessing how hard her uncle had worked to build something from scratch, she realized Joseph wasn't suggesting improvements because he thought the store was badly run. Rather, he was building on the excellent foundation her uncle had laid and she had maintained.

Joseph had said as much to her, but she hadn't understood that his vision wasn't a criticism of her management at the time.

She glanced at her uncle. His eyes were full of enthusiasm as he debated details of the quilting station. She realized her uncle's creativity hadn't waned; it was only his health that prevented him from the day-to-day running of the store. Perhaps this was the best compromise—engaging him in improvements without requiring any of the hands-on work needed to make the improvements a reality.

And she had Joseph to thank for it all.

Joseph didn't let the grass grow beneath his feet. He began the work necessary to develop the improved quilting station right away. He began by tacking up sheets and cordoning off the area with signage dramatically proclaiming: "Coming soon! Improved quilting display. Learn how quilts are made!"

He brought in some carpenters after-hours and raised partitions bracketing in the area so full-sized quilts could be mounted on three walls. He purchased a treadle sewing machine and a quilting frame from an older woman in the community who no longer wanted to sew as much. Esther donated one of her unfinished quilts to display in the frame.

Esther redesigned the order form to include a selection of patterns, colors and sizes, and put them on a stand in plain view. The forms included prices and waiting times. She contacted all the women who specialized in making quilts to see how many would be willing to work on custom orders.

Evelyn Miller, the older woman Aunt Anna thought might be interested in making packaged quilting kits for children, was enthusiastic about the idea and got to work right away.

Esther contributed a number of fabric quilting blocks, and Joseph had a sign made encouraging people to arrange the blocks into their own design. He set up a similar scaled-down display in the children's section.

And above all, he stocked the department with quilts for sale. Esther thought they had sufficient quilts in their inventory, but Joseph insisted on ramping it up. Esther coaxed additional items from the talented hands of many women in the community. These were displayed on stands or folded on shelves.

"Abundance is the key," Joseph said as he stacked folded quilts on a shelf. "The more we have on display, the more people are likely to look over the inventory."

At last, the quilting station was finished to Joseph's satisfaction.

Esther stood back as Joseph untacked the sheets from

in front of the display. It was after hours and the store was quiet, with just a few employees there closing up for the night. "After all that work, it's hard to believe tomorrow is the test of how well this will work."

"Like all things, I expect we'll get a surge of interest right away, then it will flatten out to something manageable." He bundled the sheets to one side, then came to stand next to Esther near the cash register to get a full view of the area.

He was silent a few moments, then nodded. "It looks *gut.*"

"*Ja.* Now we'll see if customers agree."

Joseph arrived early the next morning before the doors opened for the day. All the store employees were a little on edge about how visitors would respond to the new quilting station.

"What happens if we get more special orders than the women can handle?" inquired Martha. At sixteen, she was the youngest employee.

"Then we'll have to give them realistic waiting periods," Joseph responded. "Customers will have to be told these are one-of-a-kind, handmade items, not things churned out by overseas factories." He turned to Esther. "How long do you think it will take for you to make the puzzle quilt that lady ordered a couple weeks ago?"

"Keeping in mind I can only work on it in the evenings, it takes me about a month," replied Esther. "That puts me among the slowest quilters. Others can get them done much faster because they have more free time to work on them. Most of our quilters who agreed to take special orders are grandmothers who aren't busy raising children anymore."

Joseph glanced at the clock over the front door. "It's about opening time," he said. "Let's get this show on the road and see what happens."

What happened was the quilting station was a wild success. A few early customers wandered in and were immediately drawn to the colorful department, lingering over the interactive display and playing with the quilt blocks as they arranged patterns.

But when the tour buses started arriving, the interest ratcheted up to a whole new level. From her position behind the cash register, Esther watched as the vast majority of female visitors oohed and aahed over the exhibit. Most of them lingered far longer than previous tourists had stayed in the older display. And lingering, Esther knew, was a retailer's dream.

On that first day, five quilts were sold—a very high number—and the store received three custom orders.

"I'm going to portion these orders out," she told Joseph. "I won't have time to make them myself since I already have one custom order I'm working on."

"And once again, you'll be in a position where you won't keep a single one of your own quilts," he said, teasing her.

She'd told him about the paradox earlier. *"Ja,"* she agreed. "Someday I'll make a quilt just for myself."

"What will be the meaning of the quilt you keep?"

She lifted an eyebrow. "I'm surprised you remembered that. It's really amazing how much you know about quilts."

He didn't mention how much his interest had ramped up after seeing her talent. In response to her comment, he shrugged. "It's all part of being an Amish retailer," he replied. "But you haven't answered my question. If you keep a quilt for yourself, will it have a message or a meaning?"

"I hadn't thought about it," she replied. But she blushed and turned away.

Joseph wondered what that blush meant. He realized what he was hoping for when it came to Esther: forgiveness. If there was ever a theme he hoped Esther would one day incorporate into a quilt, that would be it.

A forgiveness quilt.

Because, it seemed, she was slowly forgiving him for the role he played during her painful teenage years.

And he thanked *Gott* for it.

Chapter Eight

A few days after the opening of the new quilting station, Esther was working the cash register when she noticed a pretty young woman enter the store. She had dark blond hair and blue eyes. Her dress was Plain, but she wore no kapp. She had a worried look on her face.

There was something vaguely familiar about the woman. She paused inside the store and looked around with a haunted expression, her movements quick and efficient, like a bird. But when she locked eyes with Esther, she broke into a smile.

"Esther?" she inquired, walking toward her. "Esther Yoder?"

"Ja..." Esther peered closer. "Don't tell me—Miriam? Are you Miriam?"

With a whoop of joy, Miriam threw her arms around Esther, who returned the embrace. It was Miriam Kemp, Joseph's sister and Esther's best friend from her teenage years. Esther was so happy to see her old acquaintance that tears came to her eyes.

At last, Esther pulled back and saw similar moisture in Miriam's eyes. "After all this time!" she exclaimed.

"You look wonderful! Joseph said you're a nurse now and working in the local hospital. Is that so?"

"*Ja.* I've been meaning to come by and say hello, but I've just been so busy. I love my new job. I feel so fortunate they hired me." The smile faded from Miriam's face. "I wish I had a happier reason to come in today, but I have something I need to tell Joseph that he's not going to like. Is he here?"

"*Ja*, he's in the back office." Esther felt her stomach drop to her feet. She had a feeling she knew the subject of Miriam's visit. "Come with me."

Miriam trailed behind Esther as she threaded her way among customers and displays. She looked around. "Nice place," she said. "I hear people talk about this store all the time, how popular it is and what wonderful things you sell. Now I can see why everyone raves about it."

"*Danke.* My uncle Paul started it many years ago, and I'm happy to be the manager now. It's been a bittersweet thing to sell it, but it's so much better for my uncle's health."

"What's wrong with his health? Do you know?"

"He has high blood pressure. With all the hard work he's done building this place up, it just got too much for him."

"Is he doing better?"

Esther wobbled her hand to indicate ambivalence. "He does well if he stays home and works in the vegetable patch, which he loves to do. But every time he comes back into the store, I worry about him again. He comes in every few weeks to see how things are going, and I think it tires him."

"Is he on medication to control his blood pressure?"

"That sounds like a question a nurse would ask," Esther chuckled. "No, he's not. My aunt wants him to, but he's been stubborn about it. That's why she tries to keep him from coming into the store too often and encourages him to putter in the vegetable garden, where he's happiest."

"Sounds just like a man," Miriam said, snorting with dry humor. "They're a stubborn breed."

Esther drew up to the office door, gave a staccato knock and poked her head in. "Joseph? Your sister is here."

"Miriam?" Joseph rose and came around the desk. "*Guder nammidaag*, little sister. Why are you here?" He pecked her on the cheek. "I thought you'd be at work."

"I'm heading to work right now, but I had to talk to you first."

Joseph's expression shrank into wariness. "Let me guess. Thomas?"

"Ja." Then, without warning, Miriam burst into tears.

Muttering something under his breath, he drew his sister into a chair. She pulled out a handkerchief and buried her face.

Esther lingered awkwardly. "Should I leave?"

"No, you might as well stay." Joseph spoke in a curt voice. "I don't know what kind of trouble our baby brother is in this time, but since it's bound to impact my presence here at the store, you may as well know about it."

Miriam raised her head. "It involves alcohol and a car." She hiccupped.

Joseph blew out a breath. "How bad?"

"Bad enough. He crashed into a police car. A police car, of all things!" Miriam managed a bitter laugh through her tears. "They hauled him into the station, as you can imagine. He placed his one phone call to me."

"He always does," muttered Joseph.

Listening to the exchange between brother and sister, Esther tried to keep her own feelings of dread and distrust clamped down. This, at least, didn't involve her—except, as Joseph pointed out, peripherally. But it certainly confirmed her opinion that Thomas was a ne'er-do-well who caused nothing but misery and grief to everyone around him—even as an adult. Why couldn't Thomas grow up? Why couldn't he learn self-control and personal responsibility?

"What does he want you to do?" asked Joseph.

"Bail him out, what else?" Miriam sniffled into her handkerchief.

"You're not going to, are you?"

"What else can I do? Let him rot in jail?"

"*Ja!*" spat Joseph. "Maybe it will teach him a lesson. Miriam, you can't keep coming to his rescue. That just makes it worse."

"That's what you always say. But blood is thicker than water."

"You just started a new job here—you don't need this kind of stress. You know what happened to *Daed* and *Mamm*. I don't want the same thing happening to you."

"Joseph, you know Thomas wasn't responsible for our parents' deaths."

"Maybe not *directly* responsible. But indirectly? *Ja*, I think he was."

Esther felt like fading into the woodwork. Brother and sister had apparently forgotten she was there, and she felt like an intruder into their private troubles.

"That's not fair," sobbed Miriam.

"So what do you want me to do?" snapped Joseph. "And don't tell me I should bail him out, because I won't."

"I don't have the money to bail him out," she wept. "He's begging me."

"Let him beg. Let him stay in jail." Joseph's expression was inflexible. "He has to learn, Miriam. He has to learn he can't break the law and get away with it. He has to learn he can't depend on his sister to bail him out of every difficulty."

"Besides you, he's the only one left in our family. Don't you have any pity, Joseph?"

"No. *You're* my family, Miriam. Thomas is not. I've never forgiven him for killing our parents."

"But he *didn't* kill them…"

Esther suddenly realized the heavy burden Joseph had been carrying concerning his brother. If he believed Thomas was somehow responsible for the death of his parents, that was an intolerable burden indeed. While Esther had no use for Thomas, she suddenly understood what the Bible said about the weight of unforgiveness: "Forgive, and ye shall be forgiven…"

"So you don't intend to help me, then?" asked Miriam.

"I'll help you in any way I can, little sister. You know that. But help Thomas? Not one penny. Not one."

Miriam dragged herself upright. "All right, then. I guess there's no reason for me to stay." She glanced at Esther. "I'm sorry our first meeting in so many years was like this. Let's get together sometime, *ja*? I want to hear everything and catch up on all the news."

Esther's heart contracted at the sight of her friend's tearstained face. "Of course." She stepped forward and embraced her old friend. "Anytime. And my aunt and uncle would love to see you too, of that I'm sure."

Miriam nodded, kissed her brother on the cheek and walked out.

"I'm sorry you had to hear all our dirty laundry," sighed Joseph. He dropped into the office chair, burying his head in his hands.

Esther seated herself in the chair Miriam had recently vacated. "Does Thomas always ask Miriam to help him get out of trouble?"

"*Ja.* Always." He lifted his head and leaned back in the chair. "I think that's why he followed her here when she got her job at the hospital. It drives me crazy. Miriam has worked so hard to build a respectable life and career, and Thomas is forever involving her in his shenanigans. He brings nothing but shame to our family. I keep telling her he has to learn from his mistakes, and he can't do that if she helps him, but she seems unable to stop."

"Why does she continue to help him?"

He shrugged. "I am fed up to here—" he slashed a hand across his chin "—with his escapades, but Miriam has a tender heart."

"I have no love for Thomas, as you can well imagine," Esther said. She swallowed back whatever lingering resentment she held against Joseph as well. "But I wonder if people can change? *Gott*'s love works miracles."

"*Ja, Gott*'s love can work miracles—but only if the person wants that love. Thomas doesn't. He lost his faith years ago, if he ever had it at all." Joseph wiped a hand over his face. "How can someone who grew up in the same family be so different?" he muttered.

Once again, Esther had to bite back the bile. Joseph seemed to conveniently forget his own role in her teenage trauma. He also seemed inclined to pin everything bad on his brother.

"You're determined not to forgive him," she said.

"*Ja*, you're right. I can't." Joseph's face hardened. "He's been a thorn in my side ever since we were boys, when he got into all kinds of scrapes. Now those scrapes are much bigger, more shocking, more illegal. And I'll admit, I blame the death of our parents on his behavior."

"But what does our faith tell us about forgiveness?" Esther said, persisting.

"Please don't lecture me," snapped Joseph. "You assume forgiveness is one-sided." At Esther's stricken expression, he slumped. "I'm sorry, I shouldn't have said that. As you can see, my brother brings out the worst in me." He sighed. "I once heard someone say there are four requirements for forgiveness. The first is to take responsibility for their behavior or actions. They have to acknowledge what they've done." He continued. "And remorse, true remorse. I think it's obvious Thomas is not the slightest bit remorseful."

"The other party also has to repair the damage they've done." Joseph shook his head. "Some things can't be fixed, and even if they could, Thomas isn't inclined to repair a thing."

"And lastly, repetition," said Joseph, "in which they never repeat what has happened. Thomas keeps repeating his bad choices, over and over again."

"So, you're saying Thomas is a lost cause?" she asked.

"I'm saying he's been lost for twenty-four years now," responded Joseph. "After all this time, I don't have a lot of hope." He raised an eyebrow and his tone hardened a fraction. "Why are *you* defending him?"

"I'm not. I think you know why I have no interest in defending him. But what I'm seeing is you're being eaten up inside with hatred for your brother. There's something profoundly unbiblical in that."

"On the contrary, I'm in good company. The Bible is full of stories of brothers who hated each other."

"And those stories never came to any good end," she retorted. "Look, I'm not suggesting you should bail Thomas out of his latest escapade. But neither should you condemn Miriam if she chooses to. That's her business and her conscience."

Joseph slumped in his chair. "You're right. And as you can see, I get enraged whenever Thomas comes into the picture, whether in person or in conversation. I harbor a lot of anger at him."

"I can understand why, probably better than anyone outside your family." She looked at the floor. "And forgiveness is hard. *Gott* certainly helped me when I needed it most." She added as a muttered afterthought, "No thanks to you."

"What do you mean?"

She saw genuine bewilderment in his face, and rocketed to her feet. "Never mind. I have to get back to work."

She stalked out of the office and back into the main portion of the store. Her hands were actually shaking. Automatically, she started straightening random merchandise displayed on shelves, which she tended to do when troubled.

How could Joseph be so blind to his own part in her youthful misadventure? Did he simply not remember?

Or was she not remembering the situation clearly? Could she have built a case in her mind the past seven years around incidents that didn't happen?

Painfully, she reached back in her memory to recall the humiliating time Thomas had convinced her to take off her clothes. She shuddered to think what might have happened if Joseph hadn't found them. He'd lambasted his brother thoroughly enough. But then he'd spread stories of her misjudgment and moral character to the church community to the point where Esther could no longer hold up her head.

Joseph might still disparage his brother's faults, but he simply could not see his own.

And that was the heart of the matter. Joseph refused all reasons to forgive his brother, but he didn't see the need to seek forgiveness himself. How could he possibly forget his own role in that event?

Whatever germs of personal interest Esther might have fancied she was developing toward Joseph were extinguished by his callous disregard for her own history.

Esther realized she was standing stock-still, hands clenched, glaring at an innocent kerosene lamp as if it were to blame. She took a deep, cleansing breath, unclenched her fists and walked toward the center of the store.

Forgiveness. For such a simple word, it was layered with a vast complexity of emotion. Esther knew the Bible spoke of forgiveness so many times because it was such a complicated, knotty, nuanced issue. She herself was proof of that. And at this moment, she realized she was closer to forgiving Thomas than she was Joseph.

And that hurt.

After ringing up a customer's sale and directing several others to the gardening department, Esther walked into the quilting station. She straightened out one or two quilts as she half listened to the chatter of some women admiring the handiwork of the fabric pieces.

As always, being surrounded by the beauty of the colorful fabrics calmed her down. She longed for the sanctity of her own quilting room at home, where she could forget her troubles through the medium of sewing colorful blocks into intricate patterns. Her current special-order project lay unfinished, and often her fingers itched to resume work on it even in the middle of her workday.

From the corner of her eye, she saw Joseph emerge from the back office. She turned and busied herself with some insignificant task, anxious to avoid him.

But he walked right up to her. *"Oll recht,"* he muttered in her ear. "I won't bail out Thomas, but I *will* reimburse Miriam for any expenses she incurs, if *she* chooses to bail him out."

Aware they were in public and unwilling to make a scene, Esther turned to him. "And you decided this because…?" she prompted.

"Because I'm a fool," he growled. "But as the greatest man in the world once said, we should forgive people seventy times seven. My brother is still my brother."

"We'll discuss this later," whispered Esther, as a customer came toward them with several questions.

Joseph stalked away. She thought about his capitulation throughout the rest of the workday and realized she felt ambivalent about it. Thomas was a troublemaker, and frankly she couldn't see how he could possibly overcome a lifetime of recklessness to be redeemed at his age. Part of her wanted him to stew in jail, thinking over his sins.

But every time she lingered over the thought, she found herself clenched with anger. Then she needed to take a deep breath, focus on the present, and remember Thomas was no longer her problem.

Later that evening, having successfully evaded any more private conversation with Joseph, she went home and gave a bland accounting of the day to her aunt and uncle, then disappeared into her quilting room and poured her energy into the creation before her. The custom-ordered quilt was taking shape and looked beautiful. It soothed her jangled mind to create the order and deceptive simplicity of the pattern on the table.

Even as peace crept into her soul, she knew she was avoiding confronting her own problems: forgiving both Thomas and Joseph. She had evaded Joseph after the store closed for the evening, but she sensed the subject of Thomas wasn't closed.

Not by a long shot.

Joseph ate dinner with his friends the Herschbergers, where he was renting a room, then retired to bed in a grim frame of mind. Esther's skittish and inconsistent behavior regarding Thomas preyed on his thoughts. He found himself wondering if he was jealous over his brother's influence on Esther. After all, why would she defend him, however obliquely, by urging forgiveness?

The trouble was, jealousy implied attraction. That niggle of jealousy toward Thomas made Joseph realize he himself was attracted to Esther. And attraction did not mix well with business.

Could Esther possibly still have a spark of interest in

Thomas? It certainly seemed to him as if she wanted to avoid Thomas at all costs, and she seemed grateful the time he ejected his brother from the store after he had backed her into a corner and menaced her.

But women often chose bad boys, for whatever reason. Thomas had nearly seduced Esther once before, and it appalled Joseph to think she might lean in that direction once more.

He recalled that providential moment when he had stumbled upon the two of them in the barn. Had he not found them when he did, that moment between Thomas and Esther could have been a life-altering mistake for Esther. But why had she left the community so soon afterward? He never found out.

He'd heard the rumors, of course. But he didn't believe them for a moment.

Maybe he should ask Miriam. His sister and Esther had been close friends during their teenage years, and he wondered if Esther had ever told Miriam the reason for her abrupt departure from their community.

He had to stop thinking about her. Joseph yanked some paperwork toward him, determined to concentrate on some legal documents necessary for the purchase of the store. Whatever complications his nefarious brother might cause, Joseph had no intention of backing down from purchasing the mercantile. Thanks to Paul's business sense and Esther's sound management, it was an excellent investment that he could see maintaining the rest of his life. In fact, he thought seriously about selling off his other two smaller stores he owned to concentrate all his attention on this one.

But the legal jargon on the documents blurred before his eyes, and Joseph found himself unable to focus. Visions of Esther kept rising before his eyes—backed into a corner by Thomas, knocked flat by the shoplifters, unfolding that amazing quilt she'd made, debating at dinner with her aunt and uncle about various changes to the store layout…and arguing forgiveness for his brother.

She was a multifaceted woman, that was for sure. Sometimes she blew hot, sometimes cold. Sometimes she was cool and professional; other times she was prickly and skittish. She could manage a complex store with an unruffled proficiency he had seldom seen in one so young, yet she could be completely unnerved by a careless reference to a single incident that happened years ago.

Whatever she was, Joseph found himself fascinated by her. But he wasn't sure he liked that development… at all.

Chapter Nine

"**Y**our uncle wants to go see the new quilting station at the store today, if that's all right," Aunt Anna said as she whipped up some pancake batter.

"*Ja*, that's fine." Esther sipped her tea.

"He thinks it's a wonderful idea to expand that department. He's anxious to see it."

"*Ja*, that's fine."

"He's very pleased with how well the sale of the store is coming along."

"*Ja*, that's fine."

"*Liebling*, are you *oll recht*?"

Esther looked up. Her aunt watched her with concern on her face. "*Ja*, fine. Why?"

"Because I don't think you've heard a word I've said."

Esther knuckled her eyes. "I'm sorry, I didn't sleep well last night."

"Nor did you say much yesterday evening at dinner. So I'll ask again, are you *oll recht*? Is everything okay at the store?"

"Everything's fine."

"Then why are you so quiet and preoccupied?"

Esther knew her aunt meant well, but truthfully she wasn't prepared to discuss her growing interest in Joseph, especially since it was so mixed up with resentment and bad memories and her own lack of forgiveness.

As always in times of trouble, quilting sustained her. She'd woken early this morning, seized a piece of paper and sketched out a rough idea for another pattern she wanted to try, concentrating on using her favorite puzzle-piece shapes to make a unique design. It was like reducing the art of quilting into a mathematical challenge. Mathematics was logical. It was emotionless. It didn't require forgiving.

"I'm working on a new quilt idea," she said, prevaricating. "That's where my mind has been. Do you want to see the sketch?"

"*Ja*, sure."

Esther fetched the piece of paper. "I woke up early and started drawing it out right away. I think I dreamed in jigsaw shapes," she joked, hoping her aunt would be distracted by the artwork and stop probing into her feelings.

Aunt Anna examined the sheet. "So you'll use these puzzle shapes to resemble stained glass?"

"*Ja.*" Esther pointed to the sheet. "I'm thinking, very dark and rich colors, like the sun shining through stained glass. And then, within the stained glass format, the shape of an animal or a flower or something—I haven't decided yet."

"What about a landscape scene?"

"Created with stained glass? Hmm." Esther turned the sheet front and side, examining the potential. "*Ja*, that might work. A sunset over some fields, perhaps."

"Sounds like it will be amazing." Anna smiled and turned back to the pancakes.

Esther blew out a silent breath of relief. Her aunt seemed thoroughly convinced the new quilt was at the bottom of her distraction. It was just as well.

"Anyway, your uncle said he'd be along to the store midmorning or so to see the new quilting station."

Just then, Uncle Paul bustled in with two pails of milk from one of the two cows he kept. *"Guder mariye, guder mariye,"* he rumbled. "Beautiful day out today."

"Are you sure you want to come to the store?" said Esther, teasing him. "It always sends your blood pressure up, even though you no longer have to worry about things."

"I've heard too much about this new quilting station to resist," he replied. "But, *ja*, I must admit it's a relief to turn it over to you and now Joseph. I like staying home and working in the garden." He winked at his wife. "But I'm making extra work for your aunt, since now she has so many more vegetables to can up for winter."

It warmed Esther's heart to see her uncle's good humor, as well as the gentle flirtation between the older couple. She felt a tiny ping of jealousy for their affection, which surprised her. Would she ever have a husband with whom she could joke and flirt years after their wedding?

Anna placed a platter of hot pancakes on the table. After the silent blessing, Esther speared some for her plate. "Anytime today is fine for you to see the expanded department," she told her uncle. "It's been a success so far."

"I may walk over before noon, then." He cocked his head toward Anna. "Do you want to come?"

"No, I think I'll stay home and can up all these vegetables you keep bringing in." She smiled and gestured toward a basket of peas harvested the evening before.

Half an hour later, Esther left for work, walking through the morning sunshine and thinking how fortunate her aunt and uncle were to have each other. She was glad her uncle's health seemed stabilized now that he no longer had the day-to-day responsibilities of running the store.

She unlocked the front doors, greeted employees as they trailed in and prepared for the day's influx of customers.

Joseph appeared later in the morning, and Esther was alarmed to realize her heart sped up at the sight of him. She busied herself with a task behind the cash register to hide her reaction.

"I think we're ready for some signatures on documents," he told her, leaning on the counter. "The lawyers have drawn up the papers. We can make an appointment with your aunt and uncle to go over them whenever they like."

"Uncle Paul is coming in today," she replied. "You can talk with him about when would be a *gut* time."

"Why is he coming in?" inquired Joseph, raising his eyebrows. "I thought his blood pressure spiked whenever he set foot here."

"He wants to see the quilting station. He says he's heard so much about it."

"Ain't that so? Well, *gut*. I think he'll be pleased." He traced an idle pattern on the counter. "Ah, Esther, about yesterday…"

"What about it?" She kept her voice cool and inflexible. "I don't need to hear anything more about it.

Thomas is your problem, not mine. Deal with him however you wish."

His brows drew together and he regarded her with some surprise. "I just thought you might be interested to know Miriam decided not to bail him out of jail."

That surprised Esther. "So, he'll stay there?"

"For the moment." He searched her face. "I gather he'll have a trial of some sort and then a punishment. But I don't know when that will be."

"At least we don't have to worry he'll be back to make trouble in the store, then." Curiosity got the better of her. "What was his reaction when he learned Miriam wouldn't pay his bail?"

"Not good, I hear. But I'm glad Miriam is letting him experience the consequences of his actions." He paused. "He's in the county jail, if you want to visit him."

Esther pressed a hand to her chest. "Me? Visit Thomas in jail? Why on earth would I want to do that?"

"I don't know. It's just that you seemed so...interested in his fate."

"You're mistaken." Coolness crept back into her voice. "I don't have the slightest interest in his fate." She wondered at the peculiar look of intensity on Joseph's face.

"Okay then." He straightened up and looked out the store's front windows. "Looks like the first tour bus is arriving."

The morning passed with the usual mix of assisting customers, answering questions and restocking popular items.

Around 11:00 a.m., Uncle Paul entered the establishment. He stopped just inside the door, put his hands on his hips and looked around with a smile on his face.

Almost immediately, employees came up to greet him. Esther knew how popular her uncle was among the store's staff, and it pleased her to see their enthusiastic reception.

"So this is it, eh?" He strolled toward the quilting station and stopped to examine the layout with an expert eye.

"Ja." Esther moved to stand next to him. Several customers were browsing the selection, one woman experimented with the sample fabric patches on the display table, and an elderly woman pointed out features of the quilt stand to a child.

"Very nicely done." Uncle Paul strolled around the open-sided department, hands clasped behind his back, examining the layout and inventory. Then he stepped back, all the way to the cash register, to examine the area from a distance. Joseph came to stand beside him, and he caught Esther's eye for a moment. She realized he was anxious for the older man's opinion of the expanded department.

"Couldn't have done a better job myself," Uncle Paul stated at last. "I must say, it wouldn't have occurred to me to put such a focus on quilts, but obviously, it's been the right move."

"Ja, having it so close to the front of the store is an advantage," explained Joseph. Esther heard a note of relief in his voice. "The colors are eye-catching, and we installed those side partitions to allow more full-sized quilts to be displayed, as well as to give the space a more unified feel."

Esther watched the two men discuss the merits of the addition, and it seemed her uncle was relaxed and enthusiastic.

Uncle Paul prowled around the store for a couple of hours with Joseph at his elbow. The emporium grew crowded as more tour buses arrived, and sometimes Esther had to thread her way through the crowds to answer questions or address issues. She turned over the cash register to the assistant manager.

"Esther!"

Joseph's loud voice cut through the crowd. *"Ja?"* she answered.

"Come quick!"

She darted through people, excusing herself, heading toward the tool department. She saw her uncle and stopped, horrified.

Uncle Paul was slumped on a bench, staring into space, the right side of his face sagging.

"I think he's having a stroke," said Joseph. "We need to get him to the hospital as soon as possible."

After a panicked moment, Esther's wits unfroze. "I'll call for an ambulance."

Normally, the store phone was nothing but a nuisance, but today Esther blessed the modern convenience that allowed her to call 911 immediately rather than having to hitch up a buggy and transport her uncle at horse speed.

A small crowd had gathered to stare at her uncle. Esther bit back some unkind comments about gawkers as she rushed back to Joseph. "Let's get him into the office," she suggested.

Supported under both arms, Uncle Paul was able to struggle to his feet and shuffle between them. The distance into the office seemed endless, but at last they made it, trailed by a concerned line of store personnel.

Joseph took charge. "Rebecca, you go stand out front

and watch for the ambulance. When it arrives, direct the medical team back here. John, you and Ed please watch the front door. It would be just like some people to take advantage of a medical emergency to start stealing things from shelves. Sarah, please go to Paul's house and get Anna…"

"No." Esther looked up from where she had just seated her uncle in a chair. "Don't tell her yet. We don't know the medical prognosis, and she doesn't need to worry any more than necessary."

"*Ja*, all right," agreed Joseph. He shooed everyone else out of the office and closed the door.

Esther squatted next to her uncle, overpowered by a feeling of helplessness to fix whatever was going wrong inside his brain. She forced back the tears that wanted to squeeze out of her eyes. "I've heard aspirin is supposed to help a stroke, but I don't know how much or how soon."

"And we're not precisely sure it *is* a stroke." Joseph looked just as uncertain in the face of this development. "We don't want to do the wrong thing."

The minutes seemed to tick by like hours before they finally heard the welcome wail of an approaching siren. With relief, Esther stood up.

Outside, they heard the bustle of feet and voices and paraphernalia. Joseph opened the office door just as three emergency medical personnel clattered through, loaded with equipment and pushing a gurney.

"In here," he told them. "We think it might be a stroke but aren't sure."

Esther blessed the paramedics as they took control, treating her uncle gently and efficiently. They asked him questions, listened to his heart and took his blood pressure.

"Are you next of kin?" one of them asked Joseph.

"I am," said Esther. "He's my uncle. My aunt is at home and doesn't know about this yet. I live with them, so he's like a father to me."

"Ma'am, can we bring you along to the hospital? We may need you to answer questions and sign paperwork."

"*Ja*, of course." She could barely watch as the two other responders assisted Uncle Paul onto the lowered gurney. He lay down, and they strapped him in before bringing the gurney back to waist height. Tears blurred her vision at her uncle's sagging face and weakness.

"Do you want me to come too?" asked Joseph in a low voice.

Esther realized she craved his solid strength and calm attitude. "*Ja*, please."

She followed as the medical crew pushed the gurney through the tangle of merchandise displays toward the front door. The customers were respectfully silent as they passed.

Esther caught sight of Charles, the assistant manager, whose expression mirrored Esther's own worry. She knew her uncle was well loved by the staff of the store he founded. "Please take over," she asked him. "I don't know how long I'll be gone."

"I'll pray for him." Charles choked up. "We all will."

"*Danke.*" She patted his arm and hurried to catch up with the ambulance personnel.

She waited while the medical techs loaded the gurney into the back of the ambulance, then she and Joseph climbed in and sat on small jump seats.

"Don't worry, ma'am," said one of the men. "While

I'm not a doctor, we've transported many stroke victims to the hospital. He's responsive and alert, his speech doesn't seem affected, and you didn't delay in calling for assistance. My guess is he'll make an excellent recovery."

"*Danke.* I mean, thank you." Esther sniffed and found her handkerchief to wipe away the tears. She longed to simply break down and weep but didn't want to distress her uncle further.

The town being small, it only took a few minutes to arrive at the emergency room. Uncle Paul was whisked into the depths of the hospital while Esther and Joseph were detained to handle administrative details.

"How long before we know what's happening?" Joseph asked the woman at the front desk.

She made a sympathetic expression. "It might be a couple of hours," she said. "I know waiting is the hardest part, but he's in good hands."

"Aunt Anna—I should go home and talk to Aunt Anna…" muttered Esther.

"We don't know what's happening. We'll have to wait," said Joseph. He steered her into the waiting room where a television, mounted to a wall bracket and broadcasting a sporting event, was blessedly silent.

Esther collapsed onto a padded chair and gave in to her emotions. She sobbed into her handkerchief, trying to come to terms with seeing her beloved uncle strapped to a gurney. Joseph drew her into the circle of his arm, and she leaned against his chest and wept.

After the storm passed, she pulled herself away from his comforting embrace and slumped in her chair, crumpling and uncrumpling the sodden fabric in her hands.

"Better?" inquired Joseph with brevity.

"Ja. Sorry."

"Don't be. If you hadn't broken down, it would have been me instead."

She glanced over and saw strain on his face. She nodded. "I'm going to wash up." She excused herself to the lavatory, where she splashed water on her face and tried to get her worry under control.

Two long hours passed. She and Joseph leafed through uninteresting magazines, paced around the waiting room, or watched random things on the television screen. And she prayed. Prayed hard. At long last, a doctor emerged from the double doors of the hospital.

"Miss Yoder?"

"Ja?" She whirled. "What news? Is my uncle okay?"

"Yes, he's resting comfortably. As strokes go, this wasn't bad. His speech is not affected, and since you got him medical attention within minutes, his prognosis is excellent."

Esther swayed with relief. Joseph caught her arm and braced her up. *"Gott ist gut,"* she whispered.

The doctor caught her prayer. "Yes, He is," he affirmed with a smile in his eyes. "And I'm certain that's why your uncle is doing so well."

"May we see him?" asked Joseph.

"Yes. He's settled into a room now. We'll keep him here at least two nights, but if he continues to improve, we can discharge him after that."

She and Joseph followed the doctor through the swinging doors down several corridors until they turned in a room with a single bed. A nurse, clipboard in hand, monitored a screen.

"Miriam!" Joseph exclaimed.

The nurse whirled. "Joseph! Esther! What are you doing here?"

Esther looked past her friend to see her uncle dressed in a hospital gown instead of his usual Amish clothes, propped up on the bed. He looked wan but alert, and even gave her a smile.

The doctor looked from one to another. "Do you know each other?"

"*Ja*, she's my sister."

"Yes, he's my brother."

The siblings spoke simultaneously.

"That's good, then," said the doctor. He smiled all around. "Just a few minutes with the patient, okay? Don't tire him."

"I'll make sure of it," Miriam assured him, then turned to the man on the bed. "So, this is Paul King. I didn't stop to make the connection that Esther is your niece." She laid down her clipboard and looked down at her patient.

The right side of Paul's face still sagged, making his smile distorted, but he looked more peaceful and at ease. "It's been many years, *ja*?"

"How are you feeling?" Esther sat down in the chair Joseph found for her. She leaned forward.

"A bit confused," he admitted. "I don't rightly know how I got here."

"We'll talk about that later," assured Esther. "What luck to have Miriam taking care of you. An old family friend."

"*Ja*," agreed Uncle Paul.

"The doctor—he told us you're going to get better," Esther rambled on, anxious to dispel any worry from her uncle's mind. "He said you need to stay here for a day or two, then you can go home."

"Anna, she doesn't know I'm here?"

"Not yet." Joseph stepped forward. "We'll go home after this and let her know."

"Ja, danke." Uncle Paul closed his eyes for a moment. Without warning he dozed off.

Terrified at the sight of his abrupt fatigue, she looked at Miriam, who seemed to understand her fear. She shook her head and smiled, then beckoned Esther to the other side of the room.

Esther and Joseph huddled around her in a corner. "Is it bad if he just falls asleep like that?" whispered Esther.

"Absolutely normal." Miriam kept her voice low but didn't whisper. "Sleep is the best thing he can do right now." She tapped Esther on the arm. "Don't worry, he's not going to die in front of us. The doctor is right— this is a mild stroke, more of a wake-up call than anything else."

"Going into work has caused him stress before," murmured Esther. She looked at Joseph. "This is why I'm so grateful you're buying the store. He simply couldn't handle it anymore."

Miriam looked sharply at her brother, then at Esther, then back at her brother. Esther didn't understand her friend's sharpened glances, but her own mind was so battered by the events of the last few hours that she didn't stop to analyze it.

"Ja," said Joseph. He looked over at Paul, who continued to sleep. "I think we'd best get to your house and explain everything to Anna."

"Did you come in an ambulance?" asked Miriam.

"*Ja.*"

"Then I'll call a taxi to bring you home."

Esther gave her friend a hug. "*Danke.* I'm glad you're here." She choked back more tears. "Please, take good care of him."

Chapter Ten

"How did your aunt take it?" Miriam asked.

"She was shocked, of course," replied Esther. "Though in some ways, I don't think she was surprised. She knew Uncle Paul had high blood pressure and refused to take any medicine to control it. I think she expected him to have a stroke or a heart attack someday."

Esther and Miriam sat in the hospital's cafeteria the day after Uncle Paul's stroke. Her uncle was doing much better—so much so that the doctor was confident he would be released the next day.

Miriam invited Esther to the cafeteria during her lunch break so the two women could finally have a chance to catch up.

"Aunt Anna will be here this afternoon to visit," continued Esther. "Joseph said he would drive her in the buggy so she wouldn't have to walk."

"How has it been, working with Joseph?" Miriam sipped her tea.

Esther was silent a moment. "Awkward, at first," she admitted. "I had a lot of bad memories to overcome. To be honest, when I first heard it was him who was buying the store, I was horrified. Why him, of all people?"

"It does seem ironic."

"What's ironic is how all of you, as well as myself, ended up here in the same town. I mean, what are the odds?"

"I just wish Thomas hadn't shown up." Miriam made a face.

"Joseph said you decided not to bail him out?"

Miriam's grimace deepened. "Welllll, I changed my mind. He's begging me to post bail for him."

"Won't he just get into trouble again?"

"Of course, he will." Miriam put a hand over her face. "But the thought of leaving my own brother in jail just…just…"

Esther touched her friend's hand with sympathy. "It's a difficult choice, I know."

"Ja." Miriam rewrapped her hands around her mug of tea, her face troubled. "It's this crowd he's hanging with. Some of them are doing serious crimes. To his credit, Thomas hasn't involved himself in the really bad stuff, but I worry he will at some point. Or that they may use him as a scapegoat. And you want to know my dark hope?"

"What?"

"That he finally hits rock bottom in a way that won't permanently harm himself or anyone else, and then gets redeemed."

"Redeemed spiritually or socially?"

"Both."

"Joseph wondered the same thing after you came into the store to tell us he was in jail. But he didn't sound hopeful. He said Thomas has been messing up his life for twenty-four years, so why should he change now?"

"Yet, people *do* change. They change all the time." Miriam took on an expression of anticipation. "The hospital offers all kinds of services and counseling he could take advantage of. And of course he could return to the church…"

Her friend seemed so filled with eager optimism that Esther became chilled. Was Miriam so blind to her brother's faults that she actually thought he could be redeemed? Is that why she was willing to bail him out of his latest scrape?

"Why did he turn out the way he did?" Esther mused. "You and Joseph aren't anything like him."

Miriam appeared to come back down to earth. "He's always had a wild streak," she admitted. "All his life, he just seemed to lurch from crisis to crisis."

"How does he make a living? Where does he work?"

"Surprisingly, he's a decent carpenter. He also seemed to enjoy some farming when he was younger, though I don't think he's thought of that for years. He also picked up some bookkeeping and working with computers. He's a wiz with numbers. He could do very well if he just applied himself, but he still thinks it's more fun to run around with wild people and get into trouble."

"*Ja*, but he's twenty-four. He's too old to pretend he's a *youngie*," replied Esther. "He's got to grow up at some point."

"You'd think so, *ja*. But he won't." Miriam looked down at her tea. "I think that's my hope, to be honest. That he'll realize he's no longer a *youngie* and settle down and get serious. We've all had to do that—you, me, Joseph, everyone we know. But the concept of growing up seems to have passed Thomas by entirely."

"Now what about you?" Esther asked. "You've been in town a few months now. Is there any young man on the horizon for you?"

Miriam smiled. "No. I've been so busy in my job I haven't even settled into a church. I've had one or two people from the hospital ask me out, but I've declined. I'm just not ready to settle down yet."

"I wasn't surprised when Joseph told me you went into nursing. You were always reading about herbs and healing. I'm surprised you didn't become a midwife."

"I trained for that," replied Miriam. "Someday I'd like to do midwifery full time. But for now, I like working here." She turned the tables. "But what about you? You're still single. Why?"

"Because I work too many hours," replied Esther, unwilling to delve into her private thoughts. She softened her words with a smile. "Same as you."

"What about Joseph?" said Miriam, teasing her. "He's still single."

"Why is that?" said Esther, eager to divert the topic. "He's, what, twenty-six now? Why isn't he married?"

"He was so busy with his business that I don't think he even thought about it," said Miriam. "The two other stores he bought are scattered widely, not anywhere near each other. Now there's your uncle's store, another responsibility."

"He seems very happy to be buying Uncle Paul's mercantile," admitted Esther. "In fact, he mentioned something about selling the other two smaller stores and concentrating on this one because he thinks it has the best potential."

"Ach, that's *gut*. That would keep him in town." She raised an eyebrow. "Any sparks between the two of you?"

"Plenty," retorted Esther. "But not in the way you mean. I still remember his role in trashing my reputation as a teen."

Miriam shook her head. "I still think that's very unlike him. Has he admitted to anything?"

"No, and I think that's what bothers me the most. He talks about the difficulty he has in forgiving his own brother, yet he won't own up to his own wrongdoings when we were younger. My solution is to not talk about my teenage years if I can possibly help it."

"Is it hard working with him, then?"

Esther blessed her friend's insight. "It was at first. But I think it's a sort of mutual and unspoken agreement to ignore the past and concentrate on the present. I promised my aunt I wouldn't let my personal feelings interfere with Joseph's interest in buying the store. I owe it to Uncle Paul to not do anything that might cause Joseph to change his mind. My aunt and uncle have been too good to me."

Miriam suddenly glanced at the clock over the cafeteria door. "*Ach*, I need to get back to work! My lunch break is over."

Esther wasn't too unhappy about this since she wanted to avoid any further exploration about her complex feelings toward Joseph. She rose with Miriam and went to deposit their garbage in the appropriate area.

Then Miriam embraced Esther. "Let's get together when I'm not working," she suggested. "That way, we'll have more time."

"When we're *both* not working," replied Esther with a smile.

Leaving the hospital, Esther began the walk back toward the store. Whatever her feelings about both of Miriam's brothers, it was nice to have her old friend back in her life again.

Uncle Paul was discharged from the hospital the next day. Joseph brought both Anna and Esther in the buggy to bring him home.

After all the flurry of required paperwork and follow-up orders from the doctor, Paul settled into the back seat of the buggy and sighed. The right side of his face still sagged, but not as badly as before.

"Well, there's one good thing," he quipped to his wife who sat next to him. "You've been asking me for years to get on blood pressure medication. Now I have a prescription."

"About time, too!" Anna retorted with some heat. "That's why I wanted you to see a doctor! But, no, you had to put me through all that..." She buried her face in her hands and wept.

"Ach, lieb..." Distressed, Paul patted her shoulder. He clucked soothing words as Anna sobbed out her worries and fears.

Seated next to Joseph in the front seat, Esther exchanged glances with him.

"I see why you're so relieved I'm buying the store," he murmured.

"Ja. My aunt has been worried about Uncle Paul's health for years." Esther kept her voice low, though her aunt and uncle weren't paying attention to anything else. "He poured so much energy into making it a success that I think she was worried he would keel over and die right there at the cash register."

"He has a lot of years left in him. I hope he can take it easy."

"Me too."

The ride home took less than half an hour. Joseph joined Anna in helping to support Paul on either side, as his balance was still affected. Paul slowly climbed the stairs onto the back porch and into the kitchen. "Ah, it's *gut* to be home."

"And this is where you're going to stay for a while," his wife said. "What a blessing that our bedroom is on this floor instead of upstairs. If it wasn't, we'd have to change rooms…"

Joseph winked at Esther. "I'll go unhitch the horse," he said.

"Ja, danke." Esther didn't know whether to laugh or cry over her aunt's continued fretting and unusual snappishness with her husband. "I'll make tea," she offered. Tea was a panacea in the family, a way to calm nerves and soothe tempers.

By the time the water was hot, Joseph had finished putting the horse away and returned to the kitchen, where Paul sat at the table.

Sitting down opposite Paul, he said, "Promise me you won't go back into the store. At least not for a while."

"Not to worry. I've already promised my wife." He smiled at Anna and patted her hand.

Though her eyes were still red, Anna smiled back. "Besides, he planted a huge garden this year," she told Joseph. "That means he'll be shoveling vegetables at me to preserve all summer long. He won't have time to go to the store."

"I don't think I've ever met anyone with the sense of

optimism you and Anna have," Joseph declared. "That's what pulled you through this."

"It's gotten us through some hard times," admitted Paul.

"Well, if handling the store is what sends your blood pressure skyward, at least that's something you don't have to worry about any longer."

"*Ja*, and I'm grateful, Joseph."

"Not as grateful as I am. I already told Esther I'm thinking of selling my other two businesses and concentrating on this one. I think it has that much potential."

"Now, don't *you* start getting high blood pressure," warned Paul.

"So far so good," replied Joseph, smiling. "Besides, you already did all the hard work in building and expanding the store over the years. My job now is to maintain and improve it. And Esther—" he cocked an eyebrow in her direction "—does the heavy lifting most of the time as manager."

"*Ja*. And do you know what he's making me do?" Esther kept her tone light and teasing. "He's going to make me use a *computer* to manage inventory and billing."

"Actually, we could probably hire someone to do that," admitted Joseph. "It could take a long time to learn those kinds of tasks if you've never used a computer."

"That would probably be a *gut* idea," she replied. "I have too much else on my plate to learn something that new."

Aunt Anna waved her hand to get their attention, then silently pointed at Uncle Paul. Esther looked over and saw her uncle had dozed off while sitting upright in his chair. Eyes wide in alarm, she recalled the doctor saying he needed rest and was likely to fall asleep at a moment's notice.

Joseph stood up. "Come on, Paul, let's get you to bed," he said, touching the older man on the shoulder.

"Hmm? What? *Ja*," Paul mumbled. He rose shakily to his feet, supported by Joseph, who escorted him into the master bedroom right off the kitchen. Anna followed on his heels.

A minute later, Joseph came out of the room and closed the door behind him. "Your aunt is tucking him in," he told her.

A tear leaked from the corner of her eye. "It's hard to watch him be so weak."

"*Ja*, I know. But it'll only be for a little while. He's a strong man, which is probably why the stroke was relatively mild. He needs to recover his strength and his balance, and sleep is one of the best ways to do that."

She wiped away the tear, determined to be strong as well for her aunt.

"With your uncle out of commission for the time being, who handles the livestock and the garden?" inquired Joseph.

"We both do, Aunt Anna and I," replied Esther. "We only have two cows and a small flock of chickens, so it's not like we have a proper farm or anything."

"Do you need help with the animals?"

Esther raised her eyebrows. "Are you offering?"

"*Ja*, if you need the help." He waved a hand toward the closed bedroom door. "I don't want too much pressure on any one of you right now—your uncle, your aunt…or yourself."

Esther shook her head. "We're actually *oll recht* for the time being," she told him. "We're only milking one of the two cows, the chickens don't take much time, and the garden is planted and producing well. Aunt Anna was just joking about Uncle Paul bringing her a lot more vegetables than she's used to handling. The garden is a manageable size."

"That's fine. Then if you don't need me anymore today, I'll get back to the store." When Esther prepared to rise, he said, "No, don't. Stay here and help your aunt and uncle. The store won't fall apart if you're not there for the day."

"Ja, danke." She sank back into her seat.

He touched his hat brim and walked out of the kitchen.

Esther watched him walk away, striding toward the mercantile along the familiar route she took nearly every day.

He had a cool head. A head for business, a head for a medical emergency, a head for handling details ranging from inventory to post-hospital care for her uncle. She admired that about him.

The bedroom door opened and closed behind her. She turned to her aunt. "Is he asleep?"

"Ja. I got his shoes off but otherwise just let him lay on the bed. I covered him with a quilt." Anna pinched the bridge of her nose in weariness.

Esther's heart contracted. She walked over and led her aunt toward a kitchen chair and pushed her down. Anna dropped into the seat and covered her face with both hands. Esther thought she was crying but heard no sounds of weeping. She suspected it was just bone-deep weariness.

Esther sat across the table and waited until her aunt had a chance to compose herself. Then she ventured,

"Joseph says it's probably Uncle Paul's strength that made the stroke a fairly mild one."

"*Ja*, he's probably right." Anna leaned back in the chair and closed her eyes a moment. "It's just a fearful thing to think we might have lost him."

"But we didn't. *Gott ist gut*. But now it's our job to make sure he doesn't have a follow-up stroke, and that means keeping all pressures and worries at bay."

"How thankful I am that Joseph agreed to buy the store when he did."

"*Ja*, me too." Esther kept her tone brisk and confident. "Now *aenti*, you're going to have enough on your plate taking care of Uncle Paul, so don't worry about the livestock, I'll handle that. And I can handle the garden work as well."

"On top of managing the store and working on your quilt orders?" Her aunt gave her a faint smile. "I don't want *you* to develop high blood pressure either."

"I won't. It's simply a matter of organizing my time efficiently. Watch and see."

What followed was a week in which Esther dug deep and discovered her mathematical brain had one benefit: it allowed her to precisely schedule her time to accomplish things she never knew she could do. And all she had to sacrifice was sleep.

She woke up early, spent an hour working on the quilt, often by lamplight. Then, as dawn crept over the horizon, she fed and watered the chickens, milked the cow, fed the animals, topped off their water tank and cleaned the barn.

Having delivered the pails of warm milk to her aunt, she packed herself a lunch and walked to the store. She spent the day dealing with the usual issues requiring her attention, attended Joseph when he required her participation in some aspect of the mercantile's sale, and coped with inventory and personnel.

Then she walked home and pecked her uncle on his still-sagging cheek and went out to do farm chores. She repeated the care of the chickens and cows, ate a hasty dinner and went out to the garden to weed, water or harvest as necessary, working until dusk.

Then, tired but stubborn, she lied and told her aunt and uncle she was going to bed when in fact she worked on the custom quilt that was taking shape, mostly by lamplight. She knew the sound of the treadle sewing machine wouldn't carry downstairs.

She worked until her eyes drooped, then stumbled into bed only to wake well before dawn and repeat the procedure the next morning.

She compartmentalized away her fatigue and didn't complain. Not while her uncle was showing such progress and putting on a cheerful face as he regained his strength. Not when her aunt was able to focus her attention on his health and keep the household running without worrying about outside work.

Her aunt and uncle had taken her in during a crisis in her life. She owed them her strength and industry during their own time of need.

"Are you all right?"

Esther lifted her head and realized she'd dozed off at her desk in the back office. A pile of papers—her usual hand-tallied inventory sheets—were stacked before her. Joseph stood in the doorway, watching her with concern.

"*Ja*, sorry." She scrubbed a hand over her face. "It's been a busy week."

"You look like you've been burning the candle at both ends."

"Maybe I have, but I'm getting lots done. And my uncle is improving every day." She kept her tone upbeat.

He eyed her narrowly. "Are you sure you're not doing too much?"

"I'm just doing what needs to be done." She shrugged.

"I have a feeling you're doing a lot more than you usually do, and you're not telling me about it."

"What's there to tell? Work is work."

"And sleep is sleep. How much are you getting?"

"Enough to get by." She waved a dismissive hand. "Don't fuss, Joseph. I'm fine."

"I don't believe that for an instant, but I won't push. I came in to see if you wanted lunch."

"I have lunch with me." She plucked a small insulated bag from the floor by her desk.

"No, I mean lunch in a restaurant. The same one we went to before."

She eyed him with suspicion. "Why?"

"Because you've been working so hard. Because it's a chance to discuss some business issues. And because they're having a special on chicken-fried steak, which I know you like."

The emotional wall she had constructed around her emotions chipped away a little. A chance to relax over a nice meal sounded very attractive.

She smiled. "*Danke*, Joseph. That sounds wonderful."

Chapter Eleven

The restaurant's lunch crowd had thinned by the time Esther and Joseph were shown to a quiet table in a corner. Joseph had planned it that way. He had something important to discuss with Esther—and, *Gott* willing, a seed to plant.

"See? The chicken-fried steak is the special today." Joseph pointed to a small sign on the tabletop.

"That makes my decision easy, then." Esther glanced at the menu, then closed it and smiled. "That's what I'll have. I don't know why, but I can't make a *gut* chicken-fried steak myself."

"I think I'll have the same." He also closed his menu.

The waitress took their orders, brought glasses of iced tea and placed the complimentary basket of hot cheese biscuits—for which the restaurant was known—between them.

Joseph got right to the point. "So, why are you so tired lately?" he inquired, buttering one of the biscuits.

"Just trying to keep my aunt from having to take over any of the extra chores." She pinched the bridge of her nose for a moment, then yanked her hand away.

He tried not to worry about Esther's own health. "But you said your uncle is improving?"

"*Ja.* By leaps and bounds, in fact. He cracks jokes about it, but I think the stroke scared him into realizing that my aunt has been right all these years, and he should have been taking blood pressure medication. But his balance is much better, and he's even doing a little work in the garden now and then."

"He's a tough old bird." He sipped some water. "The more I dive into the store, the more impressed I am by what he built and achieved, the vision he had and how he was able to realize that vision."

"I agree with you. It's been a remarkable education, training under him. I'm glad I was able to at least relieve him of the day-to-day tasks as he started to slow down."

Within a few minutes, the waitress brought their entrées. After the silent blessing, Esther dove into her food. "I didn't realize how hungry I was," she said with her mouth full. "*Danke*, this is a nice treat."

"So, are you more confident now about the quilting station?" he asked.

She raised her eyebrows. "What do you mean?"

"I mean, you seemed to have your doubts about it at first, but you must admit it's been very popular."

"*Ja*, I know."

He knew she was perplexed by his train of thought, but he forged ahead. "How close are you to finishing the custom quilt that lady ordered a couple weeks ago?"

"Fairly close. I've been working on it after work."

"Then I wonder if you'd be interested in another order. This came in today." He pushed a piece of paper across the table at her.

"Another custom quilt order?"

"*Ja*. It came in the mail, so the customer must have picked up an order form earlier. I think the form has all the particulars you need—size, pattern, colors, that kind of thing."

Esther studied the request. "It looks like a similar style to the one I'm making now," she remarked. "I wonder if it's not the same woman who bought that other puzzle quilt I made. The one you insisted should be displayed on the wall."

"And sold five minutes later?" He smiled. "I don't know. But it probably is. Since she's the one who bought the original, it wouldn't surprise me. As I see it, even if this person backs out of the sale, the quilt can still be displayed in the store, and it will sell that way. I'm glad we've got the quilting station set up."

Esther took another bite of her food and continued scanning the order sheet. "This is going to be a beautiful quilt," she said. "Look, the size is just right for the pattern. And she chose my favorite colors—all the earthy tones I like." Her face softened. "I could turn this into a work of art very easily."

This was going better than Joseph hoped. "All your quilts are works of art," he said. "But I didn't know size had an effect on the pattern."

"Not always, but in this case, *ja*. See how I'll pull the jigsaw blocks into a pattern within a pattern?" She tapped one spot on the order form. "Then it all comes to a pinpoint in the middle with a single block in black, with all the other colors radiating out."

"There's your mathematical mind again," remarked Joseph. "I have a fairly *gut* head for numbers, but I simply don't have your ability to translate numbers into colors and patterns. It's a gift."

"*Gott* gives us different gifts, and He gave me the gift of quilting," admitted Esther. She leaned back in her chair and took another bite of her lunch.

"How did you learn?"

"My *mamm* and *graemmaemm* taught me. And your sister and I used to spend hours working on quilts together. But I liked quilting more than any of them did, so I went further. When I came to stay with Aunt Anna and Uncle Paul here in Chaffinch, they set up one of the upstairs bedrooms as a quilting room for me. Another reason I'm grateful to them. They nurtured my skills."

"Both personal and professional, it seems," said Joseph, "since Paul trained you to run the store."

"*Ja.* He saw in me an ability I didn't even know I had. Managing the store is my job. But quilting I do for pleasure."

She glanced again at the order form, and he could almost see the wheels in her mind turning. "Let me guess," he remarked. "You can visualize what the finished product will look like, *ja*?"

"Oh, absolutely" She gave him a smile that nearly weakened his knees. "If this quilt turns out as well as I think it will, I might make myself one just like it. And keep it," she added.

"Why is it you've never made a quilt for yourself?" He sipped some water to cover his reaction.

"I don't exactly know." She traced a pattern on her plate with her fork. "Many of my quilts are custom orders, of course, but many are also gifts to friends or family, which have a meaning behind them."

"Message quilts?"

"*Ja.*" She looked at the order form once again. "This

would be the perfect pattern for a message quilt," she murmured.

Thankfully, the waitress came by with the bill at that moment, so Joseph turned to more general conversation. He was confident he had planted the right seed.

When Joseph and Esther returned to the store, it was less busy since a tour bus had just departed. But immediately, Esther noted an unusual group of men lingering in the aisles. They were not the usual type of customers the mercantile attracted. They roamed the various departments, making snide remarks about the variety and quality of the merchandise. The staff eyed them nervously.

"When did this group arrive?" Esther asked Charles.

"About twenty minutes ago." Charles watched two men as they discomposed some tools. "They're obviously not here to buy anything."

"Ah, there you are, big brother."

Esther froze, then turned around. Thomas stood there behind Joseph with a smarmy look on his face.

Joseph turned slowly to face his brother. "I thought you were in jail."

"Released, dear brother, thanks to the tender heart of our beloved sister. Now I'm able to socialize once again with my friends."

"Didn't I throw you out of here a couple weeks ago?"

"Perhaps. But I was telling my friends here—" he gestured toward the group of thuggish men who began clustering around Thomas and Joseph "—about all the fine wares you carry. They wanted to see for themselves."

The atmosphere of menace was palpable. Esther

didn't hesitate. Quietly she reached under the counter near the cash register and pressed the silent alarm button to summon the police. She had only seen it used once before, but she didn't like the look of the men surrounding Joseph.

With subtle movements, she locked the cash register and pocketed the key. She caught the eye of Charles, who nodded in approval.

One of the problems of being a Plain mercantile store was becoming the target of theft by *Englisch* thugs who knew about the Amish stricture against violence. Esther knew the store was vulnerable to exactly the kind of men Thomas had invited in.

The men now surrounded Joseph in a loose circle, focusing on him since Thomas had pointed him out. Joseph stood his ground, arms crossed, legs braced.

She resisted flinging herself in a protective gesture in front of Joseph. He would not appreciate her actions, and the men looked genuinely threatening and not above using violence against a woman.

Joseph did not back down. "I'm going to ask you and your friends to please leave."

"Aw, did you hear that, guys? He's *asking* us to leave." Thomas winked at the men. A ripple of mocking laughter came from the group.

"And what will you do if we stay here?" Thomas taunted. "Hit us over the head with your Bible?"

"Seems like a little faith might go a long way," Joseph said in a calm voice.

"Oh, I have faith, all right," jeered Thomas. "I have faith that you're a coward. I have faith that you're a fool. I have faith that you're the kind of guy who would let his own brother rot in jail rather than lift a finger to help."

Esther wiped sweaty palms down her apron. What could Joseph do against ten men looming around him? He kept his voice calm and continued to try and de-escalate the situation while Esther prayed the police would arrive.

Meanwhile, one by one, the male store employees gathered in a wider circle around Joseph and Thomas and the mob, watching. From the corner of her eye, she saw the female employees herd customers away from the action, keeping them out of harm's way. She blessed her staff, who seemed instinctively to know what to do.

The scene was certainly set for violence, and it terrified her that Joseph was in the literal center of it. She blamed Thomas for bringing his friends into the store.

And then an odd thing happened. Thomas seemed to melt away from the group, stepping into the background as a larger man took his place in front of Joseph and took over verbally taunting him. Joseph stood with his arms crossed, and Esther knew he refused to allow any temper to get the better of him.

"Coward," the thug sneered. "You don't dare lift a fist against me because you're a weakling. You're not a man."

But to Esther, it seemed Joseph was the strongest man of all, as he refused to either cower or back down, but calmly faced off against a group that seemed determined to start a fight.

In a gesture of contempt, the man flipped Joseph's straw hat off his head. It fell to the floor. Joseph continued to stand his ground as the man's heckling escalated.

Thomas, meanwhile, sauntered away and took up a position from within the tool department, watching the situation he'd set up with a smirk on his face. Es-

ther saw his expression, and in that moment, she hated
Thomas with a deep and abiding passion for setting up
his brother as he did.

Suddenly, everything happened very fast. The front
door of the store opened, and three uniformed police
officers entered. At the sight of them, the large man
who had been taunting Joseph hauled back and sucker-
punched him in the face. Joseph's head snapped and he
staggered, his nose bleeding. Esther gasped and suppressed a scream as the men scattered.

The officers sprinted after various thugs through
the store to the alarmed cries from staff and customers
alike. Stands and displays crashed and tumbled. Merchandise spilled everywhere. Several of the men made
a dash for the door, including Thomas, and escaped
outside. The officers were able to tackle and handcuff
the man who had punched Joseph, and they held two
others who struggled, but the rest got away.

Esther ran toward the back of the store, where the office and restroom were located, and grabbed a first aid
kit and roll of paper towels. As she emerged, she saw
Joseph heading her way, trying to staunch the flow of
blood from his nose.

"In here." She opened the office door. Joseph staggered in, and she pushed him down in a chair while she
yanked paper towels off the roll and began swabbing
the blood flow.

"That was brave of you," she murmured.

"Or thtupid, not thure whith," he mumbled, his voice
thick and indistinct.

She looked up as a police officer appeared in the
doorway. "Ma'am? Is he all right?"

"Is your nose broken, Joseph?"

"I don't know…" He seemed a bit dazed.

"I think it's too early to tell," she told the officer.

"We'll book this guy for assault," the officer said. "These troublemakers have been roaming the town lately. You were wise to call us."

Esther felt her throat close up. The sight of Joseph bloodied up, the fatigue from her overworked week, the knowledge that her store had been targeted by a band of hoodlums…it was all she could do to swallow back tears and try to handle things professionally.

The police officer took her report, and as Joseph recovered his wits, he told his side as well.

"My brother was among the group," he admitted, pressing a paper towel to his nose to lessen the blood flow. "He's the black sheep of the family, and he's just arrived in town. Obviously it took him no time to fall in with the wrong crowd."

"Did he commit a crime while in the store?" inquired the officer. "Theft, assault, anything like that?"

"No, not unless you consider family humiliation a crime," replied Joseph with a ghost of a smile, made more poignant by his mangled face. "He's out on bail for another crime. My fear is his behavior will escalate, and it will be just a matter of time before he does something more serious."

The officer made an expression of sympathy and confessed, "I entered law enforcement because I had a cousin that did the same thing. Fell in with the wrong crowd and started committing a growing list of crimes."

Esther bit her lip, then asked, "What happened to him?"

To her surprise, the officer smiled. "He found God, repented and became a pastor."

"Best news I've heard all day," muttered Joseph. He removed the paper towel from his nose. The blood flow had lessened to a trickle. "I just don't know if I can ever hope my brother can be redeemed."

"There's always hope." The office flipped his notebook closed. "I'll file this report. Please call if you require any more assistance." He tendered a business card.

Esther took the card. "Thank you for your fast response. The situation could have gotten much uglier if you hadn't shown up when you did."

"Ma'am." The officer saluted and left the office.

Feeling boneless, Esther pulled the desk chair opposite Joseph and dropped into it. "Does it hurt much?"

He mopped at his face, gingerly feeling his nose. "It doesn't feel great," he said, "but I don't think my nose is broken."

"I'm going to go get you a couple of washcloths soaked with cold water. You'll need to clean up before you can go out on the floor."

"Do I look that bad?"

"*Ja.* You do." She gave him a wan smile. "I'm just sorry Thomas was involved in all this."

Joseph sighed. "Not as sorry as I am. I almost can't be angry with him, even though I know his gang only came into the store because he egged them on. But I've been praying for him," he said with a note of surprise in his voice. "Praying he'll be redeemed, like the police officer's cousin."

She nodded and wondered if such a dramatic redemption was possible. "I'll get those washcloths for you, then I'd better get out onto the floor and assess the damage. You stay here."

"Don't bother, I'll just go wash up in the bathroom."

He looked down at his shirt, which had a large blood-stain on it. "But I won't be able to return to work looking like this."

"We carry men's shirts. I can bring you a clean one."

"*Ja*, maybe that's best." He squared his shoulders. "I'm actually feeling a little better now. Tender in the nose, of course, but my head is clearing."

Esther suppressed an urge to kiss him on the cheek, an impulse which surprised her. Instead she stood up. "I'll go find a shirt for you, and check out how bad the damage is in the store. It might take me a while to get back, so go clean yourself up and just rest a bit."

"*Ja, danke.*"

She closed the office door behind her and ventured out into the store, which seemed nearly devoid of customers.

"*Ja*, most of them left," admitted Charles. "I think they understood we needed to straighten things up and recuperate. I went ahead and locked the front doors and put up a note saying we were closed for an hour or so."

"That was *gut* of you."

"How's Joseph?"

"Improving. He's a bloody mess, as you can imagine, and I think the punch in the face dazed him for a bit, but he says he's feeling better. I left him to get cleaned up and told him I'd bring him a new shirt from our inventory since his is soaked with blood."

Charles nodded. "We have a good stock of shirts."

"How much damage to the store is there?" She moved toward the areas where the officers had chased down the ruffians and where most of the chaos had taken place.

"Not as much as we thought at first. Some things were broken, but most of the display units and shelves were holding nonbreakable stock," the assistant manager replied, striding beside her.

Esther saw all the store employees busy putting things to rights, sweeping up some broken crockery, rearranging merchandise on the restored display units. She joined in and, for fifteen minutes, was busy cleaning up while discussing details of the incident with the employees.

Soon Esther stood back, hands on her hips, and surveyed everything. "Thank you very much, all of you. You'd never guess anything happened by looking around. I think we can reopen now."

The employees headed back to their regular tasks. Esther walked over to the small clothing area and selected a new shirt for Joseph, then walked back to the office.

He sat at the desk, looking much cleaner. "How do you feel?" she asked.

"Better. I took some aspirin for a headache as well as the pain in my nose, so I'll survive."

"I think we'd better not mention this incident to Uncle Paul or Aunt Anna," suggested Esther. She handed him the new shirt. "It's not the kind of thing my uncle needs to know about while he's recovering."

"*Ja*, I think you're right." Joseph took the shirt. He had a brooding look on his face. "I was sitting here thinking how much my purchasing the store has caused complications, mostly because of Thomas," he said. "All these incidents—having to throw him out of the store after menacing you, and now this gang that came in… none of it would have happened if I wasn't involved."

"You can't think of backing out!" exclaimed Esther in alarm.

"No, no…that's not my intention at all. I don't think I'm expressing this well…" He dropped his head in his hands for a moment, and Esther realized he was probably in more pain than he was letting on. "But none of this would have happened if I wasn't here."

"Don't let it worry you," she told him. "What's done is done."

"I suppose." He dropped his hands from his face and stared at the clean shirt. "How much damage is there on the floor?"

"A lot less than I thought there would be. Don't let it worry you, Joseph."

He raised his head and looked at her. Though cleaner, he still looked bad. His nose was bruised and swollen, he had dark circles under his eyes. "You're a *gut* woman in an emergency, Esther. *Vielen dank* for being the way you are."

Surprised by the depth of emotion behind his words, she gave a wary nod. Then she backed out of the office and fled back onto the floor of the mercantile.

The last thing she wanted to do was fall in love with Joseph. But she realized she was in danger of doing just that.

Chapter Twelve

❧

That evening, back home with her aunt and uncle, Esther made no mention of the chaos and drama that took place in the emporium that afternoon. Her uncle looked so much better and seemed so calm and peaceful that the last thing she wanted to do was disturb him with a litany of woe.

So she put on a cheerful face during dinner and chattered about various things, then asked about the garden, a subject always dear to her uncle's heart.

"Raspberries," he said, answering her question about what was peaking at the moment. He tried to wink at his wife but failed due to the slight sag that still plagued his face. "Poor Anna has been swimming in raspberries."

"It's a good thing he likes raspberry jam, *ja*?" Anna joked back.

Seeing their familiar banter warmed Esther's heart. There were times she envied her aunt and uncle their domestic tranquility and felt privileged to have spent the last seven years watching their happy marriage at work.

A thought made her pause in the middle of the meal. Would she ever experience this kind of familial bliss?

A vision of Joseph rose in her mind, and she immediately shoved it down. She had already lectured herself about the folly of falling in love with him. She refused to entertain any such thoughts.

She suddenly remembered something and fumbled in her pocket for a folded-up crumpled piece of paper. She fished it out and unfolded it on the table. "I almost forgot—I got another custom order for a quilt today." She passed the paper to her aunt.

"That is quite a strong sideline business you've developed," her uncle remarked.

"*Ja.* I have to admit, the quilting station has brought more visibility to the quilts than I anticipated, and customers are a lot more interested than I thought they'd be."

"This looks like it will be beautiful," Aunt Anna said, studying the sheet.

"It has all my favorite colors in it, as well as that new pattern I pulled together recently. I told Joseph I might make an identical one for myself after I finish this."

"I always did think it was ironic you never kept one of your own quilts." Anna wiped her mouth and glanced at the clock. "I'll wash up," she offered.

Esther took the hint. "I'll just head out and do the barn chores," she replied. She placed the quilt order on a shelf and went out to resume her work in the barn, taking care of the chickens and the cows, then wading into the garden to weed and harvest. Her uncle was able to do more in the garden, but Esther knew how quickly things could go to waste if they were not harvested in time.

When it was near dusk, she came inside, washed up and told her aunt and uncle she was going to bed. Instead she headed for her quilting room, lit a lamp and sewed until her head nodded in weariness. Only then did she go to bed.

The next day, she woke early and forced herself to tackle her quilting project once more. Then, when the sun peeked over the eastern horizon, she went back to the barn, took care of the livestock, milked the cow and brought the foaming pails of milk into the kitchen, where her aunt was cooking breakfast.

Esther looked around the kitchen. "Where's Uncle Paul? Isn't he up yet?"

"No, he's still sleeping." Anna flipped an egg in the pan. "He's been sleeping more than normal. I thought it was something to worry about, but if you remember, the doctor said to expect it." She eyed Esther. "And don't think we don't appreciate all the extra work you're doing, both in the barn and in the garden."

Esther blushed. "I was hoping just to get the work done."

"And you are. And we appreciate it. Here, sit down and eat breakfast."

As she ate, Esther realized that her aunt wasn't aware of the extra hours she was putting into sewing, so she made no mention of it. It was not the Amish way to either boast or complain about a workload.

Afterward, she walked to the store, wondering how Joseph was feeling in the wake of yesterday's violence. He walked in shortly after opening, his face looking beaten and bruised. One eye was black, and the other still had dark circles under it. She thought he'd never looked more handsome.

"You look awful," she told him with understated irony.

"I know," he replied with more cheer than she expected. "I intend to spend the next few days hiding in the back office. I don't want to scare away the customers. Maybe I'll start setting up the inventory system on the computer."

She gave an exaggerated shudder. "Better you than me. Have fun."

The morning passed quickly. Customers came and went. Another quilt sold. At noon, she wondered if Joseph had thought about lunch since she knew it was his habit to eat out. She poked her head inside the office, where Joseph labored with a keyboard. "How's it going?"

"I hate computers," he growled.

She laughed. "Join the club. I thought you were going to hire an expert to do the transition?"

"I may have to. This is impossible to figure out."

"Did you bring lunch? Or do you want me to pick something up for you?"

He leaned back in the chair and stretched his arms over his head for a moment. Then he folded his arms on the desk. "How bad do I look?"

"Bad enough to scare a waitress. I can pick up some take-out food for you if you want."

"*Ja*. The restaurant two blocks away has *gut* sandwiches." He reached into his back pocket, removed his wallet, and withdrew some bills. "Pick up something for yourself as well."

"Oh, I brought my lunch. I usually do."

"That's the trouble with boarding with friends," he admitted. "I don't feel comfortable rummaging through their kitchen and figure it's easier just to buy lunch every day."

"*Ja*, I can see that. What do you want?"

He told her what he liked, and Esther left him to puzzle over the computer once more while she walked to the restaurant.

Returning half an hour later carrying bags of food, she knocked and entered the office. "Lunchtime."

"*Danke.* I didn't realize how hungry I was." He reached for the bags. "Why don't you grab your lunch and join me?"

She felt a quiver of eagerness, and worked hard to keep her face neutral. "*Ja*, sure."

After sitting down and both saying a silent blessing, Esther bit into her sandwich. "If you're going to stay in the area, how much longer will you board with the Herschbergers"?

"Not sure." He spoke with his mouth full. After swallowing his bite, he added, "I'm so used to being a business nomad that I haven't given it much thought."

"What do you mean?"

"I mean, I haven't settled anywhere permanently because I was too busy traveling around to the various business deals I've worked on. It seemed easier to just rent a room. But it also means eating a lot of takeout."

A thought washed through her. *You need a wife.* "But you mentioned you were interested in selling the other stores and concentrating on this one?"

"*Ja.* In fact, I've had inquiries from interested buyers, so selling them may come sooner rather than later. Both stores have made a complete turnaround in profit since I took over, and I have *gut* managers, so other business people have noticed."

"Then, if you stay here in Chaffinch, how long will you board at the Herschbergers? What will you do?"

"Probably look for a small farm somewhere. I don't

need much land, only about five or ten acres, just enough to keep a couple of cows and a garden."

"Like what Uncle Paul and Aunt Anna have?"

"*Ja.* I don't need more acreage because I'm not farming for a living, but it would be nice to have fresh food again."

Esther decided to wade into a forbidden topic. "Will you be *oll recht* settling permanently in the same town as Thomas?"

"Ah. Thomas." Joseph stalled before he could take a bite of his food. "I'm trying not to be angry with Miriam for bailing him out of jail. I haven't seen her since he got out, but I know exactly what she'll say. She thinks blood is thicker than water and believes my attitude is uncharitable."

"For sure and certain, Miriam is tenderhearted. That's what makes her a *gut* nurse. She told me..." Esther hesitated, then lurched on. "She told me she worries this crowd of men Thomas has been hanging out with may do something really awful and then try to pin the blame on him. She says her hope is he'll reach rock bottom in a way that won't permanently harm himself or anyone else, and then he'll turn his life around."

"That sounds like Miriam. Me, I gave up on that idea long ago. Thomas just never grew up, never grew out of the mean streak he had as a child and a teenager."

"That's a heavy burden for you," she said, "not forgiving."

"I've learned to live with it. But now you can understand why I get impatient with Miriam's attitude."

"*Ja*, I suppose so."

"Miriam can't understand that she must stop enabling Thomas. She holds out this desperate hope for him, but I'm a whole lot less certain."

"And this is why you can't seem to forgive him?" asked Esther. "I don't mean you should enable his bad behavior, but you can't forgive him for being a flawed human being?"

He eyed her narrowly. "You speak so easily of forgiveness. But our parents are gone because of him. How can I forgive that?"

"I know firsthand how anger can fester and create deep wounds, and how the pain continues," she said. "I see that in you now in your attitude toward Thomas."

"Did *you* forgive him for what he did to you?"

"I forgave *you*, didn't I? It took a long time, but I had to learn to forgive you for ruining my reputation when I was a teenager."

There. It was out. Joseph stared at her, baffled. "What are you talking about?"

Sleep deprivation made Esther incautious. Her voice hardened. "After you found Thomas and me in the barn that time when I was seventeen, it was your gossip—and your gossip alone—that caused me to finally leave Plum Grove and settle here in Chaffinch with Aunt Anna and Uncle Paul."

"But I thought you left town because…because…"

"Because what?"

"Well, I heard the rumors."

"You *began* the rumors, Joseph."

Joseph's eyes widened in surprise. "Hold on a second. What exactly happened between you and my *bruder*?" he blurted.

"I foolishly took off my dress." Her cheeks heated in embarrassment. "Then he took off his shirt, and then you walked in on us. Although it was humiliating, I was relieved that you prevented anything worse from happening. But then you started false rumors about what happened, and the resulting gossip was so widespread and malicious that my parents asked if I wanted to leave town and stay with my aunt and uncle." She glared at him. "The rest is history."

The rest is history. Joseph drew his eyebrows together. She acted as if he knew more than he did. "So you never...?" He paused.

"No!"

He was relieved and puzzled at the same time. "But why are you saying I started the rumors?"

"Because you did." Her voice was hard. "You passed around your terrible speculations about what happened between Thomas and me. How else would everyone have heard the fake stories? They all pointed to you as the source."

Joseph was thunderstruck. Is that what she'd thought all these years? He shook his head. "Esther, I don't know why you think I spread those damaging rumors, but it wasn't me. Gossiping is not in my nature."

"I don't believe you—but I *have* forgiven you. It was a long, hard battle on my part to find forgiveness, but I did. That's why I wonder you can't find forgiveness for your brother."

He gave an irritated flap of his hand. "Wait, go back to where I supposedly gossiped about you and ruined your reputation in Plum Grove. We've worked together now for, what, two months? Based on what you know of me now, do I seem like the kind of person who would spread rumors and trash someone's reputation?"

"I…" Esther's voice trailed off and she had a stricken expression on her face.

Into the silence, Joseph spoke. "I'd heard rumors, of course, but I can assure you I never gossiped about you, nor spread the gossip around the community. And I certainly didn't start them. As you say, gossip is a sin."

"Then—" Her voice came out as a croak. She cleared her throat and tried again. "Then, if you didn't start them, who did?"

"I don't know. It was a long time ago. All I know is when you left town, the rumors got wilder, then just died down. No one heard from you all these years except your family. We figured you just…got on with things."

He didn't mention the unspoken assumption that she had borne an illegitimate child and given it up for adoption. But he could tell Esther guessed from the way her cheeks flared red.

But her voice held dignity when she spoke. "I assure you, I 'got on with things' by training with my uncle to manage the store," she said. "Whatever other 'things' people invented were untrue. Nothing—literally nothing—happened between Thomas and me besides a teenage boy and girl's stupid curiosity. But since you were the only one who knew about the incident, since you're the one that caught us, who else could have started the rumors?"

Couldn't she see the obvious? "Thomas was the only other one there," he reminded her. "His reputation is not the best, to put it mildly. I'm inclined to pin the blame on him."

"He's a convenient scapegoat, I agree." Esther looked troubled. "But if that was the case, how could Thomas have emerged unscathed while you got all the blame? It doesn't make sense."

"It also happened seven years ago." He spoke gently. "Could your own memory be faulty? I know it was a traumatic time for you."

"I… I need to talk to my aunt." Esther's eyes brightened with unshed tears. "She remembered what things were like for me when I first showed up on their doorstep…"

A knock at the door interrupted their conversation. Charles poked his head inside. "Esther? We're having trouble with a wholesaler. Can I get your assistance?"

"*Ja*, sure." With a relieved look on her face, Esther rose.

"This isn't over," Joseph said, warning her. "I want to get to the bottom of this."

"Of course it's not over," she retorted. "I've spent the last seven years living it down. It will never be over." She left the office. Joseph stared at the closed door she had just barely managed not to slam. So she spent all this time thinking he was the one who had damaged her reputation, did she? Yet it was clear as the nose on his face that Thomas was the likely culprit. Yet another mark against his brother.

No, this was by no means over. If there was to be a future with Esther—as he hoped—he *had* to get to the bottom of it.

That evening at home on the farm, after dinner and chores were finished, Esther bypassed her usual sewing time and nabbed her aunt instead. Her uncle had retired to bed, so she and Anna had a quiet moment.

"You actually brought that up?" Anna said after Esther related that afternoon's conversation.

"*Ja.* I—I haven't been getting much sleep lately, and I think that impacted my judgment. It was making me mad to listen to him yammering about how he can't forgive Thomas for anything, when he himself never sought forgiveness from me for ruining my reputation."

"And now he says he was never involved in those rumors?"

"That's what he says. It makes me question my memory. What do *you* remember about the story when I first arrived?"

"Hmm." Her aunt lapsed into silence.

The quiet of the dusky living room was only disturbed by the familiar and comforting sound of the clock over the kitchen doorway. Esther realized her muscles were tense, braced against what her aunt might remember about those long-ago days when she first arrived on their doorstep.

"I remember you telling me about how Joseph had spread rumors," Anna said after a few moments. "But you were a little incoherent about the whole thing, and of course, I wasn't ever privy to whatever gossip was going around in Plum Grove. All I remember is how glad I was you were able to start over here in Chaffinch with a clean slate."

Esther's spirits momentarily rose at her aunt's admission but then dropped to her feet when Anna continued.

"But Esther…" Anna paused and seemed to grope for words. "*Liebling*, we love you like a daughter. You know that. But you do tend to build mountains out of molehills. The horrors you built up in your mind from that incident may not have been as bad as you remember.

We've all made mistakes. Most teenage incidents aren't held against the mature adult. If they were—" Anna smiled "—we would all be flagellating ourselves the rest of our lives. As it is written, no one is without sin."

"But…" Esther's argument died on her lips. She knew her aunt was right—she did have a tendency to exaggerate things. Or at least dramatize things.

"In other words," Anna said, "you might need to put things in perspective and move on, regardless of whether Joseph started the rumors or not."

"*Ja*, I know you're right." Esther slumped in her chair. "It's just…strange, I guess, to realize my whole adult life might be based on a faulty memory."

Anna leaned forward and kissed Esther on the forehead. "Go to bed, *liebling*. I know you haven't been getting as much sleep as you need, and I suspect your thinking is muddled right now. Pray on it. *Gott* will help sort things out."

Esther knew her bone-deep weariness was crushing her spirit. "*Ja*, you're right." She stood up. "*Danke, aenti.* You always were *gut* at keeping my head straight."

Esther went upstairs and bypassed the quilting room. She was far too tired and emotionally drained to think about sewing, especially this late into the night. Instead, she washed up and tumbled into bed.

But sleep wouldn't come. Esther put her hands under her head and stared at the dark ceiling. Could Joseph be right? Could he have had nothing to do with those rumors?

She felt like her past was a kaleidoscope. The pieces were the same, but the meanings altered as the focus shifted and formed new patterns.

If Joseph was right and he had nothing to do with

the damaging rumors that sent her fleeing from Plum Grove, then her whole adult life was based on a huge misunderstanding of his involvement in that incident. She could not continue to blame him for something he didn't do.

Nor could she take refuge in the feeling of being a victim of his gossip.

She turned over in her bed and prayed for clarity and, yes, forgiveness. Perhaps things would be clearer in the morning.

Chapter Thirteen

Esther overslept the next morning. She finally opened her eyes to bright sunlight and felt enormously refreshed. She stretched luxuriously in bed. The drama of yesterday's conflict with Joseph seemed less important and further away.

But she was running late. Motivated, she flung herself out of bed and got dressed in record time, then ran down the stairs into the kitchen, where Aunt Anna was sliding biscuits into the oven.

"Sorry, I overslept," she babbled. "I'll go milk the cow right away..."

"Don't bother, your uncle is out milking her right now." Anna smiled.

Esther drew herself up, surprised. "Really? Is he up to it?"

"He wants to try. Since his right hand was weakened a bit by the stroke, he says he can't think of a better way to strengthen it than to milk the cow. He's going slow and easy, but I think he's getting bored just sitting around the house."

"I'll go check on him, but I won't offer to help unless he needs it."

"*Ja, gut*. The biscuits should be ready in twenty minutes or so."

Jamming the final pin in her *kapp*, Esther left the house and crossed the driveway area toward the small barn. A low murmur of chatter came to her ears, and she paused and smiled. Uncle Paul was always a big one for talking to the cows as he milked.

Inside the shadowy barn, she padded over to the milking stall and leaned against a rail. Her uncle crouched on the milking stool, a bucket under the udder of the patient animal, who chewed her cud and looked content.

"*Guder mariye,*" she said. "How is the milking working out?"

"Slow," he replied, but he smiled. "But it feels *gut* to be out doing something productive."

"It's not too hard for you?"

"As I said, I'm slow. But Matilda here, she doesn't seem to mind." He gave the cow an affectionate pat on the flank.

Her heart swelled with fondness for her uncle. "I must admit, it's *gut* to see you back in the barn."

"I know it was a lot of work for you to take care of the livestock on top of managing the store," he said. "I appreciate it, *liebling*, but now I'm hoping to ease back into things."

Esther watched him fumble with the udder, his right hand clearly weaker than the left, but he compensated with patience and concentration.

"Do you want me to take care of the chickens while you finish milking?" she offered.

"*Ja, danke*, that would be fine. Tell your aunt I may be a bit longer than normal, but I'm doing all right. Just taking my time."

Esther smiled and went about feeding and watering the chickens. She knew her uncle well enough to realize milking the cow to completion was a matter of pride, a determination to overcome the results of the stroke. Besides, he loved that cow, and she suspected milking her was better than any medicine.

She reported as much back in the kitchen.

"*Ja*, I know he missed milking," her aunt agreed, turning some sausages in a pan. "I think he's anxious to feel useful again."

"I just hope he doesn't overdo it."

"Let me assure you, he won't." Aunt Anna's face took on a stubborn expression. "Or he'll have to answer to me."

Esther chuckled inwardly. She knew her aunt would keep an eagle eye on Uncle Paul. He was in good hands.

When Paul finally shuffled into the kitchen, a pail of milk dangling from his right hand, he was jubilant. "I'm going to deliberately work that side," he announced, gesturing toward the whole right half of his body. "Mark my words, I'll be right as rain inside a month."

"I'll make sure to get some raspberries picked before I leave for work," offered Esther. She strained the bucket of fresh milk while Anna put breakfast on the table.

After the silent blessing, Paul corrected her plans. "It's not too hot today. Don't worry about the raspberries, I'll pick them."

"I don't want you overdoing it."

"And I don't want to be babied," he retorted, though with a smile. "Believe me, child, your aunt won't let me overdo it. But I need to get some work done. It's healthier."

Esther agreed with him. As long as he was kept away from any strain and worry associated with the store, he was far more likely to recover in the healthy environs of a garden and his beloved cows than any other way. She made a mental vow to keep any business-related concerns to herself.

After all, the final paperwork and legal issues associated with Joseph's purchase of the emporium were nearly complete. What could possibly go wrong at this stage?

She got her answer all too soon.

Joseph opted to continue hiding his battered face in the back office. "I need to work on transitioning to the computerized inventory system," he told her, "and this way I won't scare away any customers."

So Esther spent the morning manning the floor. A tour bus had just left, and the store was somewhat quiet when she saw Miriam walk in the front door.

Normally, the sight of Joseph's sister would gladden her heart, but one look at Miriam's expression made her stomach clench. Her pretty face was drawn and tight, with dark circles under her eyes. She clutched a handkerchief in her hands and looked ready to burst into tears.

Esther went up to her at once. "You look worried."

"I am." Miriam bit her lip. "Is Joseph here?"

"*Ja*, in the back office. I have to warn you, he looks a bit battered. I expect he told you why?"

"*Ja*. And what I have to tell him will batter him even more."

Esther set her jaw. *"Komm."* She started toward the back of the store, followed by Miriam. She knocked and then opened the office door. "Joseph? Miriam is here."

"Miriam." Joseph rose and, seeing the expression on his sister's face, his own expression tightened. "Not again…?"

"Ja."

"Should I stay or leave?" Esther lingered by the door.

"Stay." Both Joseph and Miriam spoke at the same time.

She nodded and closed the door behind her, then leaned against the doorframe.

"Thomas is in jail again," blurted Miriam without preamble. "But this time for something he *didn't* do."

Joseph dropped back into his chair and shoved aside the paperwork in front of him. With irritation, he motioned for Miriam to sit on the guest chair in front of the desk. "And what *didn't* he do this time?"

"Involuntary manslaughter."

Joseph's eyes bugged. "You're kidding."

"I wish I was, but no." Miriam twisted the handkerchief in her lap. "But he says he didn't do it and had nothing to do with it. He says he's being framed."

He slammed a fist on the desk. "And I'm supposed to believe him?"

"I *do* believe him."

"Miriam, please don't take this the wrong way, but you've spent your whole life believing him. He's made a fool out of you every single time. What makes this time any different?"

Tears welled up and spilled over onto Miriam's cheeks. "I visited him in jail. He has a horrible gash on his cheek that's held together with stitches. He says he was slashed by the leader of that gang he's been hanging with, and now he's being framed. He says he was nowhere near the scene of the accident when it happened."

"Can he prove it?"

"He says he can, but we didn't have a long time to visit, so I don't know the details. He needs a lawyer, Joseph."

"And you want me to hire one." Joseph's lips thinned.

"*Ja*, I was hoping so. I… I don't have much saved up, not after bailing him out the last time."

"And after this, what next? If he's innocent, will he go on to be accused of yet *another* crime he didn't commit? When does it end?"

"Joseph, please." Miriam gave a sob, then controlled herself. "He told me he's ready to turn over a new leaf, that this made him realize he has to stop hanging around with the worst kinds of people. Just go visit him in jail. I think he's serious this time."

"What a convenient thing for him to say when he's behind bars for causing someone to lose his life."

"But he *didn't* cause someone to lose his life. The gang's leader did, but because Thomas is the new kid in the group, they figured he was the easiest guy to blame."

"That's what Thomas told you?"

"*Ja*. That's what he told me. And before you say anything more, I believe him." Miriam spoke fiercely.

To Esther's surprise, Joseph's expression softened as he looked at his sister's defiant face. In that moment, she realized how much he loved his sister.

"All right, Miriam, I'll go talk to him," he said with a certain weary resignation. "But I can't promise I'll spring for a lawyer at this point. I don't have the money, for one thing. For another, I still don't know if I believe him."

"I think you will after you talk to him." Miriam sniffed and dabbed her eyes with the handkerchief. "I think you'll find he's different. He says he wants to change, and I don't know why, but I believe him this time. I think he's scared."

"I can well imagine he's scared, but why should this cause him to want to turn over a new leaf?" He shook his head. "It just sounds like a convenient excuse to have us come to his rescue, after which he'll resume his old ways. But, *ja*, I'm willing to go see him."

"Thank you, Joseph." She stood up and walked out the office door, stopping to peck Esther on the cheek. "Goodbye."

Joseph buried his face in his hands. Esther pushed herself away from the door and dropped into Miriam's vacated seat.

"Do you want me to go with you to see Thomas?" She kept her voice gentle.

Joseph dropped his hands and heaved a sigh. "*Ja.* Probably. Otherwise, I'm likely to just lose my temper with him. And," he added, "it's only for Miriam's sake I agreed. I hold no hopes whatsoever Thomas is actually interested in turning over a new leaf. But she is always determined to see a side of him I never can. So, *ja*, having you there would probably be *gut* and keep me from telling him what I think of him."

"Believe me, I have no love for Thomas, but perhaps Miriam is right," said Esther. "If there's the smallest possibility he's being framed for a crime he didn't commit, then it's worth listening to his side of the story."

"And then what? I can't afford to hire a lawyer. They're notoriously expensive."

· "Don't borrow trouble. When do you want to go see him?"

Joseph exhaled. "I suppose the sooner, the better. I'll see if I can find out what time visiting hours are, or however it works with jail."

Esther had never been inside the county's lockup facility. The building was older, but the interior had been retrofitted with modern equipment. She felt very out of place in her Plain dress and *kapp* as she followed Joseph inside and inquired to see Thomas.

A uniformed officer led them into a room with four chairs around a wooden table. "You'll have half an hour, sir," he said.

The officer stationed himself at the door as Thomas entered from another door on the other side of the room. He wore an orange jumpsuit and looked terrified, Esther thought. His left cheek was a mangled raw mess, stitched together.

But he wore an expression she'd never seen before. Every trace of insolence had been wiped from his face and posture. He looked humiliated, humbled and, yes, terrified.

"Joseph. Esther." He sat down at the table.

Esther remained standing, but Joseph sat down opposite. "Why am I not surprised to see you here?" he asked. "What happened to your face?"

"The man who punched you decided I was a coward. He told me I needed to toughen up, and before I knew what was happening, he slashed me across the face with a knife. Told me it was a kind of initiation."

"And was it?"

"I don't care. He nearly took out my eye. That's what the doctor said who sewed me up."

"It's going to leave quite a scar."

"Believe it or not, I don't care. I've got to get out of this mess. Look, Joseph, I know I've messed up in the past, but this time I'm being accused of something I didn't do." Thomas spoke with grim precision.

"Thomas, you have a long history behind you of doing things I never liked. Why should I believe you now?"

"Because now I'm telling the truth." His voice held a strain of desperation. "I'm being framed, Joseph. I was nowhere near the scene when that man was killed."

"Miriam said you have a way to prove it."

"*Ja.* It's the only thing I can think of. The apartment complex where I live has closed-circuit television monitors in the lobby. About the time the man was accidentally killed, I was in the lobby getting a soda from a vending machine, which means I'd be recorded on those cameras. But it's probably on a forty-eight-hour loop, so those tapes have to be subpoenaed immediately, or they'll be deleted."

Esther had no idea how closed-circuit television monitors worked or how things were taped or deleted. But the urgency behind Thomas's words pierced even her armor of resentment.

"And how do these tapes get subpoenaed?" asked Joseph.

"I need an attorney." Thomas leaned forward, his hands pressed on the table. "Please, Joseph, I need an attorney to subpoena those tapes. It's the only way to prove my innocence, but it has to be done right away."

"And I assume you'll want me to pay for an attorney?"

"I don't have the money…"

"And you think I do." Joseph lashed out in anger. "You have no idea of the state of my finances, Thomas, including the fact that literally every cent I have or can borrow is tied up with the purchase of the mercantile. What makes you think I can pull thousands of dollars out of my pocket to pay for an attorney, especially for a brother who has caused me no end of trouble?" He gestured toward his own battered face. "I wouldn't have been punched by that goon if you hadn't led your gang into the store. You intimidated customers and employees alike. Now I'm supposed to fall for your sob story and shell out money for an attorney?"

Esther could hear the pent-up frustration in Joseph's voice. Unlike Miriam, she knew he'd nursed years of anger and resentment for the man in the orange jumpsuit.

Thomas slid his hands off the table and into his lap. He stared at them. "If those tapes are erased," he murmured, "there's no way I can be exonerated."

"There's an old saying, Thomas," spat Joseph. "Maybe you've heard it. You reap what you sow. You've sown years of malicious behavior to the point where no one likes you. Now, even if you're telling the truth, no one wants to lift a hand to help you."

"So, I'm doomed."

"Don't be dramatic. You're the same person. Even if you walked free today, you'd go back to your old ways, and soon enough we'd see you back in the store causing trouble."

"No." Thomas shook his head. "This is different.

I've—I've been reassessing my life, Joseph, and I realize I've got to change. Having my face slashed was a wake-up call. Maybe *Gott* is talking to me, I don't know. But this is the last straw. It's convinced me I have to change."

"How convenient." Joseph's voice held the closest thing to a sneer Esther had ever heard. "Are you surprised I don't believe you?"

"No, not surprised." Thomas raised his head, and Esther saw an expression of dignity creep into his eyes. For the first time, she saw the physical resemblance between the brothers. "What will it take to convince you I'm serious this time?"

"I don't know." Esther heard a note of doubt in Joseph's statement. "All I know is what you've done in the past must predict what you'll do in the future. It's the only standard by which I can judge you, Thomas."

"Joseph…" Thomas clasped his hands loosely on the table before him. "I know you don't think my word is much good, but let me make you a promise. A solemn, binding promise. I will rest my hand on a Bible if it will help. I promise you this. If you help me out of this mess, I will completely change. I will be a new man. I will mend my ways. I will return to the church. I will become baptized. I'm tired of living this way, Joseph, and I'm ready to transform myself into a better man. This—this attack was one thing." He gestured toward his cheek. "But this unfounded accusation is what finally scared me enough to make that change."

Joseph stared at him for a long time. "You realize, Thomas, that if I hire an attorney for you and bail you out of your current situation, if you go back on your word, I will never, ever help you again?"

"*Ja.*"

Another long silence. Esther hardly knew what to pray for—that Joseph would dismiss his brother's plea or that Thomas would truly change. Her own resentment colored her attitude toward Thomas, and a spiteful part of her, buried deep down, wanted him to stew in his own juices.

At last Joseph exhaled a long breath. "Very well. I will hire an attorney and have him subpoena those tapes. But as *Gott* is my witness, this is the very last time I will do anything for you. I will hold you to your promise. If you break it, we're through. You will no longer be my brother."

Moisture sparkled in the younger man's eyes. He bit his lip. "*Danke*, Joseph. You won't regret it."

"Time's up, sir," said the officer.

Joseph nodded and stood up. Thomas also rose. The two brothers looked at each other for a long moment, then without a word, Joseph turned to leave. Esther trailed him out the door.

Outside in the summer sunshine, Joseph slumped against a concrete planter holding a shady tree. He dropped his head in his hands. "What have I done?" he muttered.

Esther didn't know what to say, so she remained silent.

After a few moments, Joseph raised his head. His features looked drawn and haggard. "If there's a chance, even the remotest chance, he's telling the truth, I have to do this," he said.

"What if he's lying?" asked Esther.

"Then that's it. I'll never help him again. But if he's being truthful… Esther, *Gott* touched me in there. If there's a chance Thomas could be redeemed, then I must try."

"If you want to, Joseph. I won't argue. He's your brother. This has nothing to do with me."

"Actually, it has everything to do with you." He leveled his gaze on her. "The only way I can afford to hire an attorney for him is to cease the process of purchasing the store."

Stark fear drenched Esther. "No! You can't!"

She thought of the wonderful progress Uncle Paul was making in recovering from his stroke. The knowledge that the store sale might fall through could well bring on a worse stroke, one from which there might be no recovery.

"What choice do I have, Esther? I'm not a wealthy man. Everything I have is tied up in the stores. The only way to hire an attorney is to stop overstretching myself financially."

"This could kill Uncle Paul!" Her heart thudded.

"You might find another buyer…"

"How long would that take? Uncle Paul is just recovering! Any extra stress right now might bring on another stroke!"

"So you're suggesting I should just let Thomas take his chances?"

Conflicting appeals warred within Esther. Without question, her loyalty lay with her uncle's health. Her past experience with Thomas made her less inclined toward his release.

But Joseph, despite his history of frustration over Thomas's escapades, still had a strong blood tie with him. She knew he faced an ethical dilemma as well as a financial one.

Esther tried not to let rising hysteria conquer her. She fought down her panic. Berating Joseph would not change his mind. But tears rose in her eyes. She bit her lip and said nothing.

Joseph clenched his fists and turned away. "There's got to be a way," he muttered. "There's just *got* to."

Chapter Fourteen

Esther was careful not to let any hint of worry show in her face when she returned home that evening. Uncle Paul was pleased with what he'd managed to accomplish that day in the barn and the garden, and she didn't want to burden him with her troubles.

"Slow but steady, that's the secret," he told her after she'd pecked him on the cheek as always. "And it works!" His grin was lopsided, but he was cheerful.

Her heart contracted with love and pity, even as she smiled at him. "You're a tough old bird, you know that?"

"So your aunt always told me."

From the sink, Anna turned and winked at her husband.

No, the last thing she wanted to do was hint that her aunt and uncle's future security might come crashing down on them.

So she ate dinner and helped with chores and talked as if nothing out of the ordinary had marred the day. She related an amusing anecdote of a tourist who didn't believe her when she told him what a butter paddle was for. "He thought it was a garden tool!" She chuckled over the little boy who, after playing with the quilt blocks in the children's area, told his mother he wanted to make a quilt when he got home.

She filled the conversation with the normal, typical trivia of a day at work and never let on how it might all come to an end if Joseph withdrew his offer to buy the store.

At last, when Uncle Paul's head drooped with weariness, she left her aunt to put him to bed and went upstairs to her quilting room.

Only then did she unleash the torrent of fear and worry she had bottled up, muffling her weeping with a towel until it was soaked. Then she wiped her eyes, splashed her face in the bathroom and tackled the almost-finished custom quilt project with furious concentration.

When dawn lightened the eastern sky, Esther folded up the quilt. Amazing what seven hours of middle-of-the-night fury, fear and worry could do. The quilt was finished, ready to mail to the woman who had custom-ordered it.

She had a bad habit of permeating emotions into the quilt she made. This one, as beautiful as it was, felt too full of the anger and fear she had experienced while finishing it. She couldn't wait to send it off. She hoped the next quilt would be better for her peace of mind.

Esther barely felt her fatigue as she carried the quilt downstairs. The kitchen was quiet, her aunt and uncle still abed. Esther thought about milking the cow but decided to wait until Uncle Paul was up, in case he wanted to handle the chore himself. She settled on feeding and watering the livestock, then went into the garden to pull a few weeds.

Half an hour later, her aunt called to her through the kitchen window. "Breakfast, Esther!"

Esther straightened up and noted the sun had already risen. She hadn't even noticed the weeds in the bucket beside her or the reassuring twitter of birdsong. She barely heard the soothing clucks of the chickens in the pasture to the back. What was wrong with her? Nothing seemed normal this morning. She was like a zombie, going through the motions but not really present.

Lack of sleep. That must be it.

"You must have gotten up early," commented Anna, stirring some sausages in a pan, as Esther entered the kitchen.

"*Ja.* I wanted to get that quilt done." She pointed toward the finished item, then went to the sink to wash her hands. "I'm anxious to start the next quilt since it looks like it might be one of the nicest ones I'll have a chance to do."

"The one where the order was mailed in?"

"*Ja.* It's like my fingers are itching to get started on it, so I wanted to get this other one out of the way."

"Is that the only reason?"

Startled, Esther looked at her aunt. The older woman watched her with some sympathy but otherwise didn't probe.

"*Ja,*" Esther lied. "That's the only reason."

Anna nodded and turned back to the stove. Esther blessed her aunt's discretion for recognizing she wasn't ready to talk about what was troubling her.

Before leaving for the store, Esther went back upstairs to her quilting room and unfolded the order form for the new quilt. Just looking at the sketch soothed her jangled emotions. Without question, this would be one of the most beautiful quilts she could imagine. She could see the finished item gracing someone's bed—the lovely earthy tones, the complicated pattern within a pattern. Part of her eagerness to start was the implication that it would alleviate the anxious uncertainty she felt over Joseph's actions.

She sighed, placed the order form by the sewing machine, and descended the stairs to go to the store. She was not looking forward to work today. She would far rather work on the quilt.

As Joseph lay in bed in his rented room in the Herschberger home, he wrestled with his conscience and his options. He prayed. He prayed some more. But the way did not become clear.

Normally he would completely disregard his brother's plea for mercy, having heard variations on it for years and years. But this time something seemed different.

It wasn't even that Thomas believed he was being framed for a crime he didn't commit. Oddly, that wasn't what affected Joseph the most. Instead, it was the chance of genuine redemption. Joseph didn't know why, but it seemed this time Thomas was telling the truth when he promised to turn over a new leaf.

And if there was that chance his brother was telling the truth, then Joseph knew he had to give him that chance.

The lawyer he'd spoken to that afternoon after the jailhouse visit had promised to subpoena the videos from the apartment complex immediately. He had also quoted Joseph a sum for his services that made him blanch.

Joseph didn't want to withdraw from purchasing the mercantile. He considered it an excellent investment, one that he would be content to manage the rest of his working life.

More than that, he didn't want to disappoint Esther. He realized his feelings for her had gone well beyond professional admiration. At times, he found himself dreaming about the two of them on a small farm on the edge of town, a garden in back and a cow in the barn, walking together to the store. Eventually there might be children…

He shook his head and the vision disappeared. But it was just one of a number of alarmingly common images that had been plaguing him in the last few weeks.

Joseph rolled over and punched a pillow. He had done everything in his power to make sure Esther wasn't aware of his feelings. As the store owner—assuming the sale went through—he would become her boss. He didn't want to put her in an awkward position of having to refuse his interest. Joseph had been in the business world long enough to know the problems inherent in those kinds of relationships.

Besides, Esther still harbored lingering resentment over what she perceived were his actions during that incident with Thomas. All these years later, and he had no idea she thought he was the one responsible for the gossip that had ruined her reputation. Whether or not Thomas was the source of the rumors, he didn't know. But he did know Esther was not inclined to look at him kindly as a result.

And now Thomas was begging him to hire an attorney to clear his name, which would mean Joseph would have to withdraw—at least for the time being—his offer to buy the store.

How did life become so complicated?

He rose with the sun and got himself ready for work. He knew he was feeling testy, and he had to force himself to exchange pleasantries with the employees as they went about opening up the store for the day.

He headed for the office only to find Esther already sitting at the desk. *"Guder mariye."*

She eyed him and rose to her feet. He noticed she had dark circles under her eyes as if she, too, had slept badly. *"Guder mariye.* Did you, ah, make any decisions overnight?"

"I hired an attorney yesterday afternoon."

"I see." She fiddled with the strings of her *kapp.* "And what did he say?"

"He said he would subpoena the video tapes right away," said Joseph in a warning note.

He saw Esther bite her lips. "So then you've decided not to purchase the store?"

"I didn't say that," he snapped. "Everything is still up in the air at the moment, and I don't want to talk about it."

"Fine." She sidestepped the desk and slipped past him through the office door. "I need to check some inventory in the warehouse. Excuse me."

She didn't exactly flounce, but Joseph mentally kicked himself for his churlish words and irritable mood. He made a mental note to find her later on and apologize.

He dropped into the office chair, still warm from her presence, and wondered what to do.

He had no right to take out his emotions on Esther. None of this was her fault. Above all, he didn't want to do something that would damage their relationship— professional or otherwise.

Esther's excursion to the warehouse was simply a convenient excuse to allow her time to regain her composure. She returned to the store in time to see a tour bus drop its passengers off in the parking lot. She followed the crowd into the store, watching as they scattered around the various departments, chattering and remarking on the merchandise.

As always, the quilting station was popular with the *Englisch* women. Esther lingered nearby, eavesdropping on the conversations and smiling as one of her quilts was admired.

The custom quilt was tucked under the counter, out of sight of customers. "Do you want me to package up this quilt?" inquired Penny, one of her employees, as Esther returned to the cash register.

"*Ja*, please." Esther's hand lingered on the fabric for a moment, mentally saying goodbye to the project. "I think the client will be pleased with it."

Penny took the quilt away to wrap and box it, and Esther took over the cash register, forcing her mind to the task at hand.

She knew it was unworthy of her to elevate her own selfish desire to see the store sold and her uncle relieved of its responsibility, especially when balanced on the possibility that Thomas could have his soul redeemed. And so she wrestled with herself.

Suddenly, Joseph came over to her. "Esther, I owe you an apology."

"About what?"

"About snapping your head off earlier. I took my own fears out on you, and I shouldn't have done that."

She shrugged. "We're both under some strain right now."

"*Ja*, you've got that right." Joseph's gaze probed her face, and Esther wondered how visible the dark circles under her eyes were.

"Will Thomas get out on bail?" she inquired. "Will he have a trial? I don't know how these things work."

"I don't either. The attorney I hired will handle things. Essentially, it's out of my hands now." He added in a weary tone, "I think you're right—maybe it's time to forgive my brother and pray for his future."

"At the cost of purchasing the store." She made a motion as if to snatch the words back. "I'm sorry, I didn't mean to…"

"*Ja*, it might come at the cost of my buying the store. I'll do the best I can for the sale to continue, but this changes everything. But at the worst, it's only a temporary delay. From what the lawyer quoted me, it might take me a year to recoup the costs, at which point I can begin the process of buying it once again."

A year. A whole year in which her uncle, nominally, was still in charge of the mercantile. If that was the case, Esther vowed to work harder than ever to keep any pressure off Uncle Paul's shoulders.

"Why did you believe Thomas this time when he promised to turn over a new leaf?" she asked. "Hasn't he promised that before?"

"Yes and no. He's pleaded with me—well, to be fair, he's pleaded with Miriam—to bail him out of whatever trouble he gets in. Sometimes he makes vague promises to change. But being scarred by a gang leader, then accused of manslaughter—those are new ones for him. I wonder if he got scared straight, so to speak."

"I'll admit, I'm wrestling with my conscience," she said. "I don't have a reason to like Thomas, as you know. And it was a huge blow to think the store sale may fall through. So a part of me thinks we should let the chips fall where they may, where he's concerned."

"*Ja*, me too. But something was different about him yesterday. For the first time in a long time, I saw something of the little boy he used to be, before he developed the attitude problem."

Despite her anxieties, Esther relented a bit in her resentment at Joseph's change of plan for the store. Family was family, after all.

"I wonder…" she mused.

"Wonder what?"

"Your sister mentioned Thomas had some training in bookkeeping. Does he know how to use a computer?"

"*Ja*, I think so."

"If he's serious about changing, I wonder if we should give him the task of computerizing the store's inventory. I don't look forward to figuring out how to do it, and obviously you're not enjoying it either."

Joseph stared at her, seemingly poleaxed. She could almost see the gears churning in his brain. "I wonder…" he breathed. Then he collected himself and gave her a sharp look. "Why would you offer something like that?"

Was that a note of jealousy she heard in his voice? "Do you think it's a bad idea?"

"I don't know, not at this stage. I don't know if he'd be interested, of course, but I also don't know if I would trust him. He'd be setting up and then inputting a lot of sensitive information for the business."

"But if he gets it wrong, we won't have lost much since we're just setting things up. In other words, it's not like he could sabotage an existing system."

"*Ja*, true. But again, why would you offer him something like that?"

She turned away to stare at the buttons on the cash register. "Because sometimes all it takes is a chance to make a promise come true. If Thomas is promising to turn over a new leaf, maybe he needs the chance of honest work to make that promise a reality. My aunt and uncle gave me a chance like that seven years ago, and it made all the difference in my life."

"Is that the only reason?"

She glanced at him. "Yes. Why?"

"Because it occurs to me Thomas is a handsome man, or was until he got his face slashed. There might be another reason for your offer."

She stared, mouth agape. Of all the possible explanations on the planet, a romantic interest in Thomas was the last thing she had ever contemplated. "You have *got* to be kidding."

"No, actually, I'm not. Let me be blunt, Esther. Do you have an interest in Thomas?"

"Joseph, where did this come from? After what he did to me when I was seventeen, after what he's done in the last few weeks here in the store, can you honestly think I would have the slightest interest in Thomas?"

He turned to glance at some new customers walking in the front door and continued not to look at her. "It's just that a chance to computerize the store's inventory seems a rather generous offer toward a man you've always claimed to hate."

"Then forget I made the offer."

"No, don't." He turned toward her once again. "Because I think it's a good one. I just wonder at the motivation behind it."

Inside, Esther was shaking. Joseph's unexpected flash of jealousy made her wonder at his own motivation. She had schooled herself to hold him at a distance. It didn't matter if she was in love with him. Distance was better. Easier. Less complicated. And she had enough complications in her life at the moment.

"I just figured it was a way to get us out of a task we both hate," she said, improvising. "I'm not familiar with computers, and you're not much better, but it sounds like Thomas has enough skill with technology that he could pull together a computerized inventory system."

"*Ja*, he probably could."

Any further discussion was put aside as some customers came to the cash register to pay for their purchases. From the corner of her eye, she watched as Joseph risked funny looks toward his battered appearance and strolled the floor, disappearing into the building annex, where more housewares were located.

She made polite conversation with the customers, but inside she was tied in knots. She had spent so much time building a steel wall around her heart that to find it had cracks was surprising. It seemed Joseph blew hot, then cold when it came to dealing with her. She didn't want to leave herself vulnerable to the kind of emotional pain that had sent her fleeing her hometown as a teen. If she admitted she was in love with Joseph, then pain was unavoidable—especially if he withdrew from purchasing the store.

The jangle of a phone ringing cut through her introspection. She snatched the instrument off its cradle, glad for the interruption. "Good afternoon. King's Mercantile."

"I'm trying to reach Joseph Kemp," said a man's voice. "Do you know how I might reach him?"

"*Ja*, he's here. May I ask who's calling?"

"My name is Jack Bronson."

"Just a moment, Mr. Bronson. Let me put you on hold, and I'll find him."

Esther pressed the hold button and hung up the phone. She stepped away from the cash register and went in search of Joseph.

She found him chatting with a male customer over the merits of some gardening tools. Walking up to the pair, she waited a moment for a pause in the conversation, then said, "Joseph, you have a phone call."

"Excuse me, please," he said to the man, and turned to follow Esther. "Who is it?"

"Someone named Jack Bronson."

He stopped in his tracks.

Surprised, she asked, "What's wrong?"

"He's the businessman interested in purchasing one of my smaller stores."

A wild hope made her heart thump. "Why would he be calling here?"

"That's what I'd like to know."

He strode toward the back of the store and disappeared.

If this Mr. Bronson was interested in purchasing one of Joseph's smaller stores, could that mean he would not have to pull out of the deal to purchase Uncle Paul's store?

She paused inside the cash register corral, closed her eyes and prayed.

To her surprise—and annoyance—Joseph didn't stop to talk with her after the phone call ended. Instead he grabbed his straw hat, jammed it on his head and left the store.

Esther was flooded with anxiety. Joseph's face didn't look optimistic as he departed. What could that man have said on the phone?

Chapter Fifteen

❧

That evening at home, Uncle Paul kept up his cheerful and optimistic outlook. "Picked a gallon of raspberries today," he gloated. "And your aunt made some jam."

"He's steadier on his feet too," said Aunt Anna. "Every day is an improvement." She beamed at her husband.

How could Esther interfere with this kind of recovery? She vowed not to mention anything negative until it was impossible to avoid.

Instead, she excused herself early to go up to her quilting room. "I'm anxious to start this next quilt," she explained.

"*Ja*, go." Aunt Anna flapped a hand and smiled. "I know how much you love sewing."

Esther climbed the stairs and entered her special room. The late afternoon sun spread a golden glow across the bolts of colorful fabrics. She selected the colors requested on the quilt's order form, spread the cloth across the table and started cutting.

She worked with assurance and speed since she knew the pattern and technique now. The work left her mind free to think, to hope, to pray.

And she prayed hard. At the moment, there was nothing more important to her than her uncle's health.

Joseph sat opposite the desk from Stan Wheeler, the attorney he'd hired on behalf of his brother. The office had walnut furniture and plush carpets. Sourly, Joseph wondered how much of the money he was paying the attorney would go toward nicer furniture and plusher carpets.

But there was no question this attorney was one of the best in town. He came highly recommended.

"The videos clearly show your brother in the lobby of the apartment," Stan explained, stabbing a finger at an iPad on the desk between them. "See? The time stamp shows he couldn't possibly have been where the man was killed." The attorney leaned back and steepled his fingers.

"So you think Thomas was being framed?"

"It seems so, but I'm still pulling together the time table. I'll be honest, Joseph, this evidence is strong, but your brother may still have to go to trial."

Joseph winced. A trial would only increase the cost of Thomas's defense. "But why would it go to trial if this video shows my brother wasn't anywhere near the scene of the crime?"

"It may not. I'm just warning you it's a possibility. It depends on the judge."

Joseph shook his head. He'd never understood the *Englisch* legal system, but then he'd never had much interaction with it either. "Does Thomas have to stay in jail, or can he be released on bail?"

"He'll stay locked up. But one thing you may not

know—the leader of that gang he's been hanging with has also been arrested on an unrelated charge."

"Is he the one who punched me in the store?" Joseph gestured toward his face, still discolored from the blow he'd received.

"No, it's a different guy. This group is not a proper gang, since thankfully we don't have gang activity in Chaffinch. It's just a group of loosely affiliated men who like to cause trouble. Like your brother," he said.

Joseph winced. "I hope he's serious about turning over a new leaf," he muttered.

"I'll do what I can to move things forward. If the judge thinks this evidence is enough to clear Thomas, your brother may get released within a day or two. If the judge thinks there's more to it, he may request a trial."

Joseph suspected the attorney was deliberately simplifying the situation for him, since he understood so little of the legal system. That was all right with him. He wasn't sure he wanted to learn anything more about criminal justice than he had to.

Joseph rose and reached over to shake the attorney's hand. "Thank you for doing what you can to help my brother," he stated. "If you need to reach me, you can call the mercantile. I'm there most of the time."

He left the law firm and strode down the street, eyes on the sidewalk, praying the phone call he'd received earlier that afternoon would bear fruit. Jack Bronson had said he was definitely interested in purchasing one of the two smaller stores Joseph owned. The process was likely to be a slow and thorough one, since he knew Bronson was a careful businessman. But the sale of the store would more than pay for the attorney fees incurred to clear Thomas's name.

He just wished he could move things along faster. There was a lot at stake—especially his future with Esther. If he had to stop the process of purchasing her uncle's mercantile, it would alter his status in town.

But if all went well…he intended to court her.

Esther cut and sewed long into the night. She was too keyed up to sleep. The pieces of fabric formed into quilt blocks under her skilled fingers, and even by lamplight, she could tell the blend of colors and shapes would make a unique and beautiful whole.

And while she worked, she prayed. Prayed for her uncle's continued recovery. Prayed Joseph would be able to complete his purchase of the store. And she even prayed for Thomas's redemption.

The latter surprised her, and she realized she had forgiven Joseph's rapscallion sibling for his part in launching her into her current situation. She realized she had grown strong as a result of the teenage scandal, whereas Thomas had grown weak. Forgiveness, she now realized, was another measure of strength.

As always when she sewed, she felt like she was imbuing the fabric under her fingers with the emotions she felt. It seemed the quilt she was making would be a forgiveness quilt, and as the colors and patterns took shape, she longed to keep it for herself rather than send it off to an unknown customer.

But that wasn't practical. She made quilts to sell them, not keep them.

And Joseph… Esther's fingers quivered over the cloth pieces. She realized that while her admiration for the man had ripened into love, she didn't want him to know that. If he bought the store, he would be her employer. If the sale fell through, he would leave town. Neither option was conducive to the kind of solid relationship like her aunt and uncle shared.

So she would keep her feelings to herself.

It was long past midnight by the time she finally blew out the lamp and tumbled into bed. Despite the late hour, the work had calmed her. The future lay in *Gott*'s hands, not hers. She would face whatever came with calm maturity.

"So that's what Jack Bronson told me." Joseph folded his hands on the desk.

Sitting opposite him in the back office of the store, Esther felt a leap of hope. "So your ability to purchase this store essentially hinges on whether this Mr. Bronson can purchase your other store?"

"*Ja*, that's the gist of it. The attorney fees won't be due right away, and the attorney already told me I could set up a payment plan. If the other store sells, then I can pay the entire amount off right away. If the store doesn't sell…" His voice trailed off.

"I understand." Keeping to her promise to face the future with calmness and maturity, she kept any hint of worry or disappointment from her voice. "I won't say anything to Uncle Paul or Aunt Anna until we know one way or the other. We're young enough to bear the burden of worry for them."

He looked at her with an unfathomable expression. "*Ja*, we are. *Danke*, Esther. Now all we can do is sit and wait."

Outwardly, she faced the future with calmness and maturity, but over the next week, Esther felt eaten up inside with worry. Joseph left on a business trip to meet with Jack Bronson at his other store location elsewhere in Indiana, and she missed him more than she ever thought she would.

So she poured heart and soul into her quilt, which took shape with astounding speed.

"It's lovely," sighed Anna, when Esther invited her to see the work in progress. "I wish I had your skill and vision, child. What a pity you can't keep this one."

"I know." Esther smoothed a hand over the quilt top. The project was ready to go into the quilting frame to be joined with decorative stitches to the batting and bottom. "I don't know who ordered this quilt, but I hope they appreciate it as much as I do. I think *Gott* had a hand in designing it."

Anna leaned against the doorframe. "How long until Joseph gets back from his business trip?"

"A few days, I think." Esther busied herself with pins and thread. "He just had to talk to that possible buyer for the other store and go over the books with him."

Her aunt and uncle knew about the potential sale of Joseph's other property but knew nothing about the urgency behind it—nor of Thomas's situation.

"Do you miss him?"

"Who? Joseph?" Startled, Esther stared at her aunt.

"Ja." Anna wore a compassionate expression. "I have eyes, child. I can see you have feelings for him."

"Oh." Esther stilled her fiddling. "I didn't think it was obvious."

"Sometimes the things we deny are obvious to everyone but ourselves. Does he return your interest?"

"I don't know. He's never said anything."

"It sounds like you've forgiven him for his part in ruining your reputation seven years ago."

"*Ja*, I guess I have." Esther smoothed the fabric in front of her. "I don't know how I feel about him, Aunt Anna. It's complicated."

"These things usually are. Don't fret, Esther. *Gott* is in control. Leave it in His hands."

"Oh, I already have." She looked up at her aunt with a faint smile. "I have no other choice, do I?"

When Joseph reentered the store a week after he'd left, she saw in a moment he bore good news.

"He's interested," he said without preamble, a big grin on his face.

It was all she could do from squealing and throwing up her arms in glee. "Does this mean you won't withdraw your offer to buy this store?"

"For the moment, no. I'll see how this goes, but it seems *Gott* is offering a solution for all of us—you, me, Thomas and your uncle."

"I haven't heard what's happening with Thomas in the week you've been gone. What's the situation?"

"He's been released on bail and is back at his apartment, but I don't know the details." He paused. "But he did ask if we could come see him. Apparently, he has some things he wants to say."

Esther went still. "We? As in, both of us?"

"*Ja.*"

"I understand why he wants to talk to you. But why me? Why would he possibly want me there?"

"I don't know. But, Esther, I'm asking you to come."

Startled, she looked at him. He looked back with an expression that made her heart flop. *Does he return your interest?* her aunt had asked about Joseph. Before, Esther wasn't sure. But now...

"I'll go," she replied.

* * *

Thomas lived in a small apartment building on the far edge of town. It was on the seedy side, with shabby landscaping and peeling paint. Joseph pulled the horse-drawn buggy to a stop in front of the unit. "Where can I hitch the horse, I wonder?"

Most businesses in town provided hitching posts for the convenience of the Amish population, but this building was the exception.

"Over there, maybe?" Esther pointed to a shady tree across the street.

"*Ja.* I've got an extra rope, so I can tie the horse to the tree trunk." He directed the animal forward.

Within a few minutes, she and Joseph approached the door. Esther wiped down the palms of her hands on her apron as Joseph knocked.

Thomas opened the door. He wore a faded brown shirt and jeans. The stitches were gone from his cheek, but the wound looked red and ugly. He didn't give his insolent smile. He didn't look arrogant. He merely stepped back and said, "Come in."

The inside of the tiny apartment was dingy and dark, with minimal furniture. The only places to sit were chairs around a small kitchen table.

Esther seated herself, facing her old adversary with reluctance. But just as he appeared when she last saw him in jail, he was subdued and quiet.

The brothers each sat down as well, but Thomas said nothing.

"So why did you ask us both here?" Joseph prompted, when Thomas seemed unwilling to talk.

"I… I hardly know where to begin." Thomas clasped and unclasped his hands on the table. "It's been a rough couple weeks, as you can imagine."

"The video footage exonerated you from the involuntary manslaughter charge?"

"*Ja*. And more than that, the guy who did it stepped forward and confessed he tried to frame me. I'm a free man."

"That's *gut*, then." Joseph paused. "So, why did you want to talk with us?"

"I've… I've been thinking things over a lot. Jail will do that, I guess. There's nothing to do *but* think." He continued to wring his hands. "The leader of the group I've been hanging around with…well, he always poked fun at me and called me naive because of my Amish background. I realize now he took advantage of that to try and pin a very serious crime on me."

"And nearly succeeded." Joseph's voice was stern.

"*Ja*. And I realized I could be in prison for a death I had nothing to do with if I didn't get away from them and straighten myself out. It scared me, Joseph." Thomas's eyes suddenly swam with tears. "I've always envied you. Even when we were kids, you were the competent older brother, the guiding light, and I wanted to be nothing like you. But now I look back at my life and begin to see just how useless and worthless I've been. You became a businessman. Miriam became a nurse. Me? I became a criminal."

Joseph leaned back in his chair, and Esther saw an expression of wary acknowledgment on his face. "I can't argue with you," he said.

"Nor should you. But I wanted to tell you this. The promise I made in jail is a promise I intend to keep. You've bailed me out for the last time. I aim to return to the church and hope to be baptized. I'm going to find a steady job and stick with it. You did the right thing in helping me this time, Joseph, and you won't regret it."

Joseph let out a low whistle. "If you're telling the truth, Thomas, then we can credit *Gott* with this."

"As we should. I've ignored *Gott* for many years. Maybe all my life. But I realize He never gave up on me, He still wants me, even though I spent my whole life making a mockery of His wishes. That's going to change."

"Then this buyer was an act of *Gott*," Joseph muttered.

"What buyer?"

"I was on the verge of withdrawing my offer to buy Paul's store, because otherwise I couldn't come up with the money to pay your attorney. But I may have a buyer for one of my smaller stores. He seems very serious. The sale of that store would pay off your legal fees without affecting the current business deal. I see the hand of *Gott* in all that."

Thomas's shoulders wilted with relief. "*Ja.* And I give you another promise, Joseph. I will pay you back. It will take me some time to get on my feet financially, but I will pay you back."

"Don't. Pay it forward instead."

"What do you mean?"

"Just that. Someday you're going to come across someone who needs help. Pay off your debt to me by helping them."

A gleam of hope crossed Thomas's face. "*Ja,*" he said softly. "I will do that."

Throughout this exchange, Esther sat in silence. While she was glad to witness the reconciliation between the brothers, she wondered why Thomas asked her to be present.

Her question was answered when Thomas looked at her and said, "And Esther, I also wanted to apologize to you for what happened when we were teenagers."

She stiffened. "That was a long time ago."

"*Ja*, it was. But what you may not know is Joseph had nothing to do with the rumors that followed, though I made it seem that way. I was the one spreading the rumors. It seemed kind of fun at the time, or at least fun from the perspective of the snarky horrible teenager I used to be. I didn't think how badly it would impact your whole life."

Esther sat stunned. In one brief moment, her whole perspective shifted, like the kaleidoscope she had imagined before. The pieces were the same, but the meanings altered as the focus shifted and formed new patterns.

Thomas was responsible for everything. Joseph had nothing whatsoever to do with ruining her reputation. It all made sense.

"Now I understand," Thomas continued, "what it's like to have someone trash a reputation like I trashed yours. The consequences could have been far more severe for me, but that doesn't mean the consequences to your reputation were any less earth-shattering. And for that, Esther, I want to apologize from the bottom of my heart."

"All these years…" she breathed. "I thought Joseph was responsible."

"Another one of the big sins I've committed in my sad and sorry life," Thomas said. "I wanted to lay everything on the table. I've wronged you both in more ways than I can even count."

Emotion was high in the room as the years of misunderstandings and wrongdoings were aired. More than aired—forgiven. Esther hadn't understood how the burden of hate she carried for Thomas had weighed her down. The act of forgiving him didn't just lighten the atmosphere; it lightened her soul.

Thomas and Joseph talked, but she barely heard them in the haze of her thoughts. When she finally dipped back into the conversation, she realized Joseph was addressing practical considerations of employment. "Then what will you do for a job?"

"I don't know. This apartment is paid until the end of the month, but I'm going to have to find regular work. It's been years since I've done any of the things I trained in—bookkeeping and carpentry and construction—but maybe I could find something along those lines…"

Joseph glanced at Esther, and she read his mind. She gave a tiny nod.

"Esther had an idea," Joseph said. "We're in the process of computerizing the store's inventory system. Neither of us has more than a passing familiarity with computers, but you've had more experience since you've been out in the *Englisch* world for so long. Would you be interested in the job?"

Thomas's jaw dropped. He stared back and forth between them. His throat worked. "You would do that for me?" he croaked.

"*Ja.*" Joseph nodded. "It would help all of us, I think."

Thomas's eyes filled with tears. "*Gott* had his hand in all this," he said, choking out the words. "I can see that now, plain as day. Why did I spend my whole life denying that?"

"You have a long road ahead of you," Joseph said.

"*Ja*, of course I do. But I'm anxious to get started. There's an old cliché that says a journey of a thousand miles starts with a single step. I want to take that step."

Joseph patted his brother on the shoulder. "You already have, Thomas. Welcome home."

Chapter Sixteen

"Oh, *liebling*, it's beautiful." Anna examined the finished quilt with an air of authority. "I think this is one of the nicest you've ever made."

"*Ja*, I agree." Esther stroked the fabric. "This will be one quilt that will be hard to part with. After I send it off to the customer who ordered it, I'm going to make another one just like it, this time for myself."

The coverlet that spread out on the table was more than just a collection of fabric and stitches. As with so many of her quilts, Esther felt this one was imbued with the emotions she felt while sewing it. Those emotions had been rampant with the relief of forgiveness in the aftermath of Thomas's redemption.

More important was the relief of knowing Joseph had nothing to do with the rumors that had ruined her teenage years. Seeing him in this new light altered her feelings about him. At the moment, those feelings took the shape of vague hopes she didn't dare verbalize.

With some reluctance, Esther folded the quilt and slipped it into the bag she reserved for transporting her projects to the store. "I'd best get to work."

"How has Thomas been doing with the computerized inventory?" asked Aunt Anna.

"Amazingly well. He's so anxious to do a *gut* job that he's been putting in long, long hours. He works a computer very well, far better than Joseph does, and certainly better than I do."

"Gott ist gut," said Anna. "He brought another lost sheep home."

"Ja. I'm glad to see forgiveness within the family. Miriam is so happy her brother turned around."

"Sounds like she's the one that had the faith he'd change all along."

"Ja. She saw something in him Joseph completely missed. That I missed too."

When Esther arrived at the store before opening, as usual, she was surprised to see Joseph already there. His voice echoed in the otherwise deserted building. A ray of early sunshine pierced the gloom of the building in which the lights were not yet turned on.

"Gut news," he told her. "Jack Bronson does indeed want to purchase the store. In fact, he might purchase my second store as well. That would leave me free to concentrate on this one."

"Oh, Joseph, that is *gut* news indeed!" She beamed at him. "I know you were under a lot more stress than you were admitting."

"Ja," he agreed. "And I think you were right not to mention any of this to your uncle while he's recovering. I'm glad he's doing so much better."

"Me too," said Esther in a heartfelt voice. She heaved the bag with the quilt onto the counter.

"So this is it?" Joseph touched the bag. He sounded

nervous all of a sudden. "This is your custom order? May I see it?"

"Ja." She slid the bag off the fabric and unfolded it, draping the quilt across the counter, where it spilled down the side. Though the full effect of the pattern wasn't possible from the rumpled arrangement, the earthy colors gave it a rich beauty. "I fell in love with this quilt. I'm going to make an identical one and actually keep it this time."

Joseph stroked the fabric. "I've never met anyone as skilled as you."

Compliments were rare things among the Amish. Esther stared at him. *"Danke,"* she replied in an uncertain voice.

He continued to finger the quilt. "Esther, there's something I should tell you. The customer who ordered this quilt? It was me."

"You?" Her voice scaled up. "You're the one who placed the order?"

"Ja."

"But…but why? It's not normal for a man to want a quilt."

"Because I knew what you wanted. You told me the pattern and colors you love, and I wanted you to have a quilt for yourself."

Esther had a hard time meeting the intensity in Joseph's eyes. "Then I can keep it? It's mine?"

"Ja. It's entirely yours."

She caressed the fabric. In a low voice, she said, "In some ways, this quilt has a message. It's like the emotions I was feeling while making it became part of the fabric. I'm glad to keep it for those feelings alone. I think of it as a forgiveness quilt."

"That's funny, I was thinking of it as a marriage quilt."

She caught her breath. "What do you mean?"

"I mean, I hope to see it gracing our marriage bed someday." The ray of sunshine which pierced the gloom of the store highlighted the expression of hope on his face.

Her heart started beating in slow, painful thuds. She breathed, "Joseph, what are you saying?"

"I'm saying I love you, Esther. We've been through a lot over the past few months, both professionally and personally, and through it all, I grew to admire everything about you." He touched the quilt. "My hope is that you'll say yes, and this will be our marriage quilt as well as a forgiveness quilt."

Esther's eyes filled with tears. *Gott* had heard her prayers.

"Ja," she whispered. *"Ja*, a thousand times over!"

He reached out and embraced her. Esther laid her head against his chest and heard his heart beating fast.

By the time employees started filing in and going about opening the store to the public, Esther had packed away the quilt and tucked it in the back office. Suddenly the glorious project was too personal, too intimate, for anyone else to see. Anyone except Joseph.

Joseph. She emerged from the office onto the retail floor and caught his eye. She bit back a smile, hugging herself with happiness.

He came over to her. "I feel the same way," he told her over the chatter of voices. "This November, we'll be together forever."

November was the traditional month for Amish weddings. "I can't believe it," she replied. "It's like a dream come true."

"I'd better stay away from you, or our secret will be out in no time." He grinned. "And no one is supposed to guess, *ja*?"

Another Amish tradition. Courtships were conducted clandestinely.

"Ja." She turned away, trying to keep the glow of happiness off her face. But it wouldn't be easy.

Joseph carried the bagged quilt in his arms, walking beside Esther through the warm August evening toward Paul and Anna's house.

"Is it my imagination, or does the whole world look golden?" She gestured toward the sunbeams through the tree limbs.

"It does seem pretty golden," Joseph agreed, smiling at her.

She caught her breath at the love in his eyes. *"Ja,* golden," she breathed.

They found Anna on the front porch sweeping away the day's dust. "Joseph! How nice to see you. Can you stay for supper?"

"Ja, I'd like that." He lowered the bundle onto the porch. "Ach, that's heavy."

Anna stared at the bag. "Esther, is that your quilt?"

"Ja." She grinned.

"But I thought you were shipping it to the customer who ordered it. Did they change their mind?"

"Well, there's a story behind this. I can tell it over dinner." She wanted to dance and caper with the excitement of telling her aunt and uncle the news.

"Well, come in. Dinner should be ready in a few minutes."

Joseph picked up the quilt and followed the older woman into the house.

Uncle Paul sat in the living room, reading the day's newspaper. Esther kissed him on the cheek.

"Gut'n owed, liebling." Her uncle smiled. "And *gut'n owed*, Joseph. Everything all right at the store?"

"Ja, just fine. Great, in fact."

Paul leveled a thoughtful glance at Joseph, and Esther wondered if he guessed the news.

While Joseph stayed to chat with Paul for a few minutes, Esther carried the quilt upstairs to her sewing room. She flirted with the idea of spreading it out on her own bed but decided against it. This quilt was special. It was her marriage quilt.

It wasn't until everyone had gathered around the table and the blessing over the food was already said when Joseph paused. "I believe the man who bought one of my stores has plans to purchase my other small store," he stated. "With that lump sum, I should have enough to buy a small farm nearby. Nothing big, maybe about the same size you have here."

"That will be nice," commented Anna. "I can't imagine it's pleasant, renting a room in someone's house for months on end."

"Ja," Joseph agreed. Under the table, he squeezed Esther's hand. "You should also know about the quilt," he added. "It was a custom-order quilt...from me."

"From you?" Anna's eyes widened. Her hand, poised to ladle soup into a bowl, remained suspended. "You ordered a quilt? Why?"

"Because I knew Esther would love it. This way, she gets to keep it for herself."

"Ach, liebling, that's lovely!" Anna's face glowed with a smile. She put the ladle down in the soup bowl.

Uncle Paul looked at Esther with amused suspicion.

"So you finally get to keep a quilt. Does this mean what I think it means?"

She smiled at the man who was like a second father to her. *"Ja,"* she said simply. "Joseph and I are getting married."

Anna sucked in her breath and clapped a hand over her mouth, her eyes moistening. Paul broke into a grin and clapped Joseph on the back. "That's *gut* news!"

Esther sighed in utter contentment. "I thought I was making a forgiveness quilt," she admitted. "It turns out I was making a marriage quilt."

"About time too." Joseph winked at her.

Epilogue

Joseph wrapped his arms around Esther's waist from behind and rested his chin on her shoulder. "It looks wonderful," he murmured.

"*Ja.* It does." Esther was nearly breathless with admiration.

The storefront before her was small but lovely, part of a line of brick retail spaces from the turn of the century located directly across the street from King's Mercantile. The setting sun twinkled on the windows, which displayed an assortment of beautiful and eye-catching quilts. Inside the store were hundreds of bolts of cotton fabrics in every color and print imaginable, along with thread, batting, pattern books, kits and various notions and tools. Cheerful cloth bunting was nailed up across the awning, framing the store's name—The Quilting Bee—welcoming visitors to the store's grand opening.

"This way, I'm not competing with the mercantile by selling quilts," observed Esther. "But I get to indulge myself in my passion all day long as well as encourage other quilters." She hugged his arms around her waist. "Oh Joseph, it's like a dream come true."

He dropped a kiss on her neck. "You've trained Charles so well to take over management of the store that it should be smooth sailing, even without you. And now you can apply your considerable talents toward your own business. But I warn you," he said teasingly, "Don't make any more quilts like the one on our bed. That one is too special."

"Agreed. Our marriage quilt is one of a kind."

His arms tightened. "Just like our marriage."

* * * * *

Dear Reader,

I hope you enjoyed *The Quilter's Scandalous Past*, following Esther's story of forgiveness. It illustrates how important it is to let go of grudges and find the best in people.

It's also a story of how mistakes from our adolescent years don't necessarily carry over into adulthood. For that, I think every one of us can be grateful. Esther has a skill I admire passionately—quilting. My sewing skills atrophied when I was about eight years old, and now it takes an act of Congress to get me to stitch fabric. As a result, my admiration for those skilled in the needle arts is second to none.

Are you curious what happens to Thomas? His story is told in my next book, *Their Road to Redemption*, to be released in July 2023.

I love hearing from readers and welcome emails at patricelewis@protonmail.com.

Patrice

COMING NEXT MONTH FROM
Love Inspired

HIS FORGOTTEN AMISH LOVE
by Rebecca Kertz

Two years ago, David Troyer asked to court Fannie Miller...then disappeared without a trace. Suddenly he's back with no memory of her, and she's tasked with catering his family reunion. Where has he been and why has he forgotten her? Will her heart be broken all over again?

THE AMISH SPINSTER'S DILEMMA
by Jocelyn McClay

When a mysterious *Englisch* granddaughter is dropped into widower Thomas Reihl's life, he turns to neighbor Emma Beiler for help. The lonely spinster bonds with the young girl and helps Thomas teach her their Amish ways. Can they both convince Thomas that he needs to start living—and loving—again?

A FRIEND TO TRUST
K-9 Companions • by Lee Tobin McClain

Working at a summer camp isn't easy for Pastor Nate Fisher. Especially since he's sharing the director job with standoffish Hayley Harris. But when Nate learns a secret about one of their campers that affects Hayley, he'll have to decide if their growing connection can withstand the truth.

THE COWBOY'S LITTLE SECRET
Wyoming Ranchers • by Jill Kemerer

Struggling cattle rancher Austin Watkins can't believe his son's nanny is quitting. Cassie Berber wants to pursue her dreams in the big city—even though she cares for the infant and his dad. Can Austin convince her to stay and build a home with them in Wyoming?

LOVING THE RANCHER'S CHILDREN
Hope Crossing • by Mindy Obenhaus

Widower Jake Walker needs a nanny for his kids. But with limited options in their small town, he turns to former friend Alli Krenek. Alli doesn't want anything to do with the single dad, but when she finds herself falling for his children, she'll try to overcome their past and see what the future holds...

HIS SWEET SURPRISE
by Angie Dicken

Returning to his family's orchard, Lance Hudson is seeking a fresh start. He never expects to be working alongside his first love, single mom Piper Gray. When Piper reveals she's the mother of a child he never knew about, Lance must decide if he'll step up and be the man she needs.

LOOK FOR THESE AND OTHER LOVE INSPIRED BOOKS WHEREVER BOOKS ARE SOLD, INCLUDING MOST BOOKSTORES, SUPERMARKETS, DISCOUNT STORES AND DRUGSTORES.

LICNM0423

HARLEQUIN
PLUS

Try the best multimedia
subscription service for romance
readers like you!

Read, Watch and Play.

Experience the easiest way to get
the romance content you crave.

Start your **FREE TRIAL** at
www.harlequinplus.com/freetrial.